STRONG POINTS

VICTORIA D G
ALBERTU

To Sally with love –

ROY STRONG

Strong Points

Drawings by Ian Mackenzie-Kerr

Roy Strong

Thames and Hudson

Printed and bound in Great Britain by
The Bath Press, Bath, Avon

Contents

Times and Tides

Word for Word

The Swish of the Curtain

Foreword

These short essays were written for *The Times* between August 1983 and February 1985. The subjects were all of my own choosing, with the exception of the first essay, 'My Perfect Day', which was commissioned for a series. As well as being reflections on a period, they embody, I hope, a certain way of looking at things.

I would like to thank Peter Stothard for giving me the enjoyable opportunity to write these occasional pieces.

ROY STRONG
February 1985

My perfect day

IT IS TRUE to say that one is only aware of a perfect day in retrospect. As the light fades and there is a faint nip in the air and the dinner seems especially fine, the mind reaches back over the day and, like God in chapter one of Genesis, concludes 'It was good.' It is particularly good if the experience is a shared one, although this is not a totally necessary ingredient.

Nearly everyone, if pressed, would admit that their most perfect days are not in the least exotic but positively humdrum. They are composed at their best of a combination of everything one loves most, set into a perfect accord.

In my case it would stretch from being awakened by the loving purr and lick of a tortoiseshell cat, to a stroll around the garden with my wife and the shared contentment of realizing that this or that really is more beautiful than last season. It would embrace a happy period in one's writing room when the words would flow; reclining in the bath listening to the radio; and a session in the kitchen that produced memorable results. In other words, tranquillity of a kind found in a drawing of a *biedermeier* interior. For true happiness in life, perfect days should be a combination of the attainable within the boundaries of one's own existence.

But there is another form of perfect day – strange, imaginary, even fantastic, in which one shapes the hours from sunshine to shade into a sequence of precious, memorable and pleasurable experiences.

Such an exercise almost defies decision. It would demand far more than the requirements of he who defined heaven as eating foie gras to the sound of trumpets. It would have to embrace a choice between so many contraries: the music of Mozart and musical comedy; the first flowers of spring and a bottle of Pouilly Blanc Fumé; the voluptuous decadence of Strauss's

Rosenkavalier and the pious words of the Book of Common Prayer; the cool magic of Piero della Francesca's *Madonna del Parto* and the taste of raw herring as it arrived on the quayside at Scheveningen. The list would be formidable and impractical but if practicality of a kind is to govern these twenty-four hours they would run something like this . . .

The day would have to begin in a four-poster bed. In fact I'd have to start in England somewhere, in a great house. I would have arrived in the dark because one of life's pleasures is to wake up in a strange room and find a completely new world revealed through its windows.

To wake and find myself master of Hardwick Hall or Knole would suit me admirably as a start to the day. Both are very well off for sumptuous beds, especially the latter, and I'd be happy in any of them, all standing in rooms with evocative names: the Spangle Bedroom, the King's Bedroom and the Venetian Ambassador's Bedroom.

Let me decide definitely in favour of Knole, for although I find Virginia Woolf and the 'Bloomsburys' tiresome, her description of that house in *Orlando* is a distillation of the allure of such a mysterious, rambling, old mansion, thick with dust and heady with the emotions of centuries. To awaken there would be quite something – to suddenly feel attentive fingers heave back the silver and gold curtains, to peer out of the window and glimpse courtyard and parkland and grazing deer.

It would definitely have to be autumn, one of those golden, slightly hazy mornings with light piercing cloud and mist. Late September ideally, when the leaves would just be beginning to change to red and gold; promises of warmth at noon but also a certain hint of sadness and decay at the season's end.

There is nothing more irritating about staying in a great house than having to go down to breakfast. No, I would leap from bed and put on the garment I covet most in the Victoria and Albert Museum's dress collection: Mr Coutts's dressing gown, a regency confection of mock ermine in wool.

I don't know whether Knole has marvellous bathrooms, but for a perfect day perfect plumbing is essential. And in any case the bath is one of the best places in which to look at pictures. My own is filled with nondescript prints but to be really perfect the Mauritshuis gallery in the Hague would have lent Vermeer's *View of Delft*. It would be perfection to me but no doubt sacrilege to others to lie back in a scented tub contemplating the picture I'd rescue first in the world. What pleasure to have that huge sky to oneself, with its extraordinary patches of light falling on town and water, utter peace and calm with those six figures standing on the quayside.

After this, a continental breakfast certainly, in terms of the best coffee and bread, although preserves by the Women's Institute I would regard as a *sine qua non*.

Hopefully, Mr Tommy Nutter would have delivered something appropriate to wear, for clothes add spice to life. I would be quite happy wandering alone through the rooms and galleries of that enormous house, pausing at faces and china; sniffing old pot pourri; lifting swags of faded velvet; sitting on the Jacobean chairs; sensing in short everything that is England. Perhaps the sound of Elgar's Symphony No. 1 in A flat would echo through the walls and one would tiptoe into the chapel to hear another music, that of the Authorized Version read in a place where John Donne preached and the formidable Lady Anne Clifford 'blubbered with weeping'.

But away, melancholy, for this perfect day is drifting towards the valedictory. The garden at Knole is not much good and I would have to get to a garden somehow, either Hidcote or Cranborne Manor, which depend on rooms and topiary of box and yew, statuary and pergolas, and herbaceous borders laden until the blooms cascade on to the connecting paths.

Which brings me to lunch. I remember a wife years ago in a post-war film asking her husband, 'Proper lunch or proper dinner?' Lunch is a pretty expendable meal except in the vanished form of the luncheon party, but then that would eliminate three hours from my perfect day. I'd compromise with a picnic beneath the greenwood tree: Japanese food and *sake* with Jean Muir, David Hockney and Zandra Rhodes. It's about time this perfect day began to be populated and they would make up an hilarious and observant party, stylish, perspicacious, unserious yet serious, reticent yet eccentric and outgoing.

My Knole mood of grandiose melancholy would be sent up on sight and the day would gain wit and momentum, ingredients essential to its coming hours, for we should all be gathered up in a happy haze and wafted by the most luxurious means possible to Italy. We would avoid all those things that make air travel pure hell: tickets, luggage, checking-in, passports, even the duty free.

I confess freely to the Englishman's obsession with Italy which set in from the moment that I first cast an eye on the Lombard plain in 1955. It would have to be part of a perfect day somehow, but how?

Domesticity is a great thing and I would round everything off with the perfect Italian complement to Knole, Palladio's Villa Maser. It would have to be evacuated and given over to us in every sense and the weather would need to be warm and serene, for here would be staged the one most perfect meal of the day at a round table placed at the crossing of its elegant galleries. Candles everywhere would softly light Veronese's fantasy world as he opens walls and ceiling out into landscape and up into a pagan heaven. The table would be covered with damask and lace trailing to the floor; everything would be white with only flecks of gold and silver and the food would be served on flower-sprigged porcelain.

A little Mozart would be in order here, I feel, to match in delicacy the food: caviar, smoked salmon, lobster, fish from the lakes – a marine banquet with the best champagne. And everyone would dress up marvellously for the sheer fun of it, although I still remember David Hockney's remark to me more than a decade ago when I descended for dinner looking like an *incroyable*: 'Have you done your act yet?'

And why this place? In one building, a home in the country, it epitomizes in wood, stone, brick and paint the civilized values of the Renaissance, that golden age of European man, at its most optimistic. Man the microcosm is the measure of its proportions and here was a house conceived not only for happiness but work and philosophical contemplation. Its decoration is at once light-hearted and deeply profound. The *trompe l'oeil* doors are swung open to reveal a hunter returning with his dogs, a little girl peeping in and a page hastening to answer a call. The frescoes celebrate the beauty of landscape and the gift to man of wine and love. But at its heart stand grave ladies making silent music with their instruments. Near to them pikes, halberds and lances lean against painted Corinthian columns.

From our dinner table we would see war vanquished by the arts of peace in a setting that evokes all that Western civilization at its very best has achieved and stands for. One could not ask for more: good company, delectable food, music, laughter and happiness within one of the supreme environments created by the hands of man.

Design
for
living
Bath
Salts
MR

John Piper

Passages and Corridors

Table-laying

Packets and Labels

Window Dressing

Biedermeier Revived

Bathrooms Old and New

Postcards

Fashion Observed

John Piper

JUST BEFORE the last war my late mother-in-law's nanny had a farm outside Henley from which 'a nice young Mr Piper' used to give her lifts into town. That marked my wife's first awareness of the artist John Piper.

Mine was that of a generation which grew up on King Penguins and Penguin Modern Painters. Among the former was a volume, published in 1950, dedicated to the Romney Marsh, with watercolours of landscapes and buildings already executed in that idiosyncratic alliance of crayon, wash and ink which Piper developed over the years as his particular vehicle for interpreting the countryside. The book on Piper in the latter series came out earlier, in 1948, and included two of the great series of Windsor Castle, commissioned by the Queen Mother during the war, which now adorn the library at Clarence House and of which legend has it that George VI remarked 'I'm sorry that you had such bad weather, Mr Piper.'

I was also hypnotized by one of his earliest theatre designs, for the ballet *The Quest*. I remember Doris Langley Moore later telling me she had to concoct a patriotic plot in order to get Ashton out of the RAF to choreograph this – and what better source than Book One of the *Faerie Queene*.

These are early impressions made on an adolescent by an artist who has now passed his 80th birthday. There can have been few so prolific in this century, literally thousands of drawings, paintings, graphic works, as well as stained glass, photography, ceramics and theatre design. What small verse can I possibly add to the hymn of praise now arising?

What I wish to sing about may seem a small and very insular thing, Piper's very Englishness. The work of other giants of his generation – Moore, Hepworth, Sutherland or Nicholson – could, in the main, be plonked down anywhere. They are products of international modernism. Their imagery and iconography have been less tempered by the vast literary and visual heritage of their own country. Piper has never turned his back on that and, to a degree, has, as a result, suffered in the esteem of fashionable critics. And always he has loyally remained with us and never become an expatriate. How could he when all around lie the sources of his inspiration?

Without doubt he will go down as the greatest exponent of the English topographical tradition in this century. Through his art he has given vitality and life to a form that seemed mummified in the format of its forbears or outmoded by photography. As it is, his drawings and paintings of English churches and their interiors, landscape and coastline, great houses and their gardens have taught more than my generation not only to look at our past through other eyes but to appreciate and care for it. They are works of art about works of art. They are simultaneously elegies and polemics. The principles of the modernist movement have been assimilated and applied but never at the expense of the innate visual conservatism of the British.

In this respect his long joint editorship of the *Shell County Guides* with John Betjeman should not be forgotten. In many ways they now seem old-fashioned in approach but they do represent an attempt to look at the visual fabric of the country in a way different from the art historian's applausometer which forms the least attractive aspect of Pevsner's mighty series, *The Buildings of England.* The Betjeman-Piper approach is romantic and historical, totally un-Germanic, in fact rather dilettante and literary. And, as in the case of the topographical work, this forms a peculiarly English way of looking at things.

I shall always remember my first glimpse of John and Myfanwy Piper in the early 1970s. It was a golden late summer evening. As we approached the flint farmhouse, they sat together on a wooden bench at a table on which Myfanwy was shelling into an earthenware crock peas that John (a brilliant gardener) had grown. On the table stood glasses and a bottle of wine from the Sitwell castle of Montegufoni. Over their heads was a huge old bleached sunshade. It was a scene so simple, domestic and totally unaffected, speaking of security and serenity but with a respect for the innate nobility of common things typical of Stubbs. To me it summed up all that was most true in the art of John Piper.

Passages and Corridors

WHEN IS a corridor a passage, or a passage a gallery? The question is arguable, except that one generally knows when experiencing it. I have always had a romance about strolling through these apparently useless parts of a building, useless, that is, apart from connecting point A with point B. All this was called to mind when mounting a postcard in a scrapbook of one of my favourite corridors (too narrow to be a gallery, too grand to be a passage) in Frederiksbourg castle, outside Copenhagen.

About seven feet wide, it crosses the moat and leads to one great room, which in itself is rather a disappointment. The corridor, however, is not so, with its late seventeenth-century mullioned windows on either side and the rippling reflection of water on the scrolled plasterwork of its walls and ceiling. At each end the doors are marked by looped curtains in plaster and the walls are inset with paintings in the Russian manner, apart from which everything is monochromatic, marble, marbling and shadowplay.

The Grand Corridor at Windsor Castle takes the prize as the greatest British passage, wide and bending its way around a large part of the castle, like a broad Garter sash linking *grands* and *petits appartements*. Its mystery lies precisely in that awkward bend, thus always giving anticipation of new marvels as yet unperceived as Gainsborough gives way to Winterhalter banked on its walls. Unlike Frederiksbourg, this regal passage is not cool in mood but lush, enveloping the voyager in crimson and gilt.

I suppose the real test as to whether a corridor is or is not a gallery is the degree to which it is utilitarian. The Grand Corridor fulfills that criterion, as does another favourite, *Il Corridoio*, linking the Uffizi and Pitti palaces in Florence. It is a rare privilege to walk the meandering mile of this supreme passage superimposed on to a city.

Il Corridoio is often very ungrand. Beginning held aloft by columns, it soon becomes a workaday passage with portholes which suddenly give out on to the Arno as one crosses the Ponte Vecchio, and then, on the other bank, there comes a touch of drama as doors to one side are flung back and we find ourselves in the gallery of Sta Felicità, looking down onto the enamelled surface of Pontormo's altarpiece.

If we cross the narrow definition which divides the corridor from the gallery I confess to being haunted by the one at Sabbioneta in the Casino del Giardino. One can truly define that building as a gallery with a palace attached. It has the contradictory element of simultaneously being seen at a glance, a sweep of immense length, and yet taking ages to walk from one end to the other. Pure Renaissance in its symmetry and adorned with faded grotesque-work frescoes, the walls are pierced on both sides by windows which enable light to stream into it at all times of day. The impact is hypnotic.

I suppose if I had to criticize the long gallery at Hardwick Hall it would be precisely because it had windows only on one side and at the ends. But then I know of no other place where pictures are hung directly over tapestries, a throwaway effect which still makes every visitor draw a breath. Our own long galleries have a peculiar magic, particularly when it seems as if the other rooms have been disposed merely as pendants to this vast, unoccupied, rectangular space. It is when the staircases, as, for instance, at Montacute or Chastleton, wind their way ever upward only to deposit one at the gallery that the effect is unforgettable. And the entrance is always rather a mean one through the panelling at the side, which again emphasizes the effect.

When a gallery becomes galleries and when a corridor becomes corridors, joy is extinguished. The experience has to be unique in a building for wonder to be sustained. Just the sight of the *Grande Galerie* in the Louvre or the mileage of the Hermitage sinks the senses. Marvels they contain, of course, but I am left with a Kafka-esque feeling of depression otherwise aroused in the case of the corridor only by those in hotels and government offices. Unwindowed and dimly lit, they stretch into the distance, flanked by doors concealing one knows not what.

Extraordinary it is that such seemingly trivial spaces can exert such power over us, as a sensation of exaltation passes all too quickly to one of fear. One has every sympathy for poor Alice . . .

Table-laying

CHRISTMAS is one of those occasions when even the most run-of-the-mill households pause and attempt to essay one of the arts of living, table-laying. Recently Lady Clark told me how, when she was busy in the kitchen preparing lunch, her husband would go out into the garden in search of the 'bouquet' for the table. 'Please remember *not* to pick those two irises,' she would ask, but he always did, demonstrating exactly his appreciation of the aesthetic of the table.

There is a marvellous museum in Stockholm which exhibits the history of table-laying. Down a darkened corridor the visitor goes past room after room laid in period style, one a ladies' dinner held in a bedroom by a roaring fire, as in the engraving by Abraham Bosse, another evoking the naughtiness of the *ancien régime* with Sèvres porcelain arranged for a meal *à deux* at a table whose cloth trails to the ground, knotted at the corners. What art the consumption of food has evoked – but always mosaic pieces to be rearranged and reset to capture mood and ambience, from banquet to buffet.

My recollections of memorable tables would form an eccentric list. It would not be particularly governed by splendour at all. It would include a humble lunch of cold meat and salad with Duncan Grant at Charleston. The painted wood table, the pottery, even the food was pure Omega workshops. John Piper's honest scrubbed wood table at Fawley matches it in another way, for from the centre arises a bank of white pottery candlesticks, all sorts and sizes, with cascades of dripping white wax. Artists' tables are always interesting, because they naturally approach them as a form of still life.

No reminiscence of memorable tables can exclude grand ones however. So many of these are a letdown. A ton of antique silver is not necessarily beautiful. The Royal Academy dinner is positively municipal when it ought to be a visual feast. To it might be applied a remark made to my wife, a short time ago, at another grand table. Looking at the explosion of 'All-the-year-round chrysanthemums' in the middle, her neighbour commented: 'I assume that these will be sent to Golders Green immediately after.'

A state banquet at Buckingham Palace provides one of the last glimpses of table-laying in the grand manner. The menu lists the glorious porcelain from which the guests eat, and little cards reveal the antiquity of the vista of candelabra and epergnes that stretch in each direction. On that occasion cascades of *alchemilla mollis* revealed the delicate restraint of whoever orchestrated this spectacle. How different from a luncheon by an American millionaire, where the museum accession numbers on the plates were noticeable. Nothing like eating off your tax concessions.

Eating is a wonderful opportunity for looking, and not only at flowers and artefacts from the past. Modern ceramic sculpture produces delightful pieces to enliven a table. Bryan Newman's evocation of old London Bridge and John Gandy's garden wall topped by urns and peacocks have given me endless pleasure. One of the sad aspects of the dining table at 10 Downing Street is the total absence of any contemporary ceramics or silver. There table-laying ought to be a celebration of this country's past and present creativity.

The most memorable table I ever had to arrange was a luncheon party for the Queen Mother at Ham House. The table was placed as it would have been in the time of the first Duke of Lauderdale, in Catherine of Braganza's bedroom, with the Royal visitor sitting so that the garden's lines of perspective met in her eyes. I regret to say that a colleague's bed was despoiled of its lace counter-pane, and statuettes of the seasons were ferried down from the V & A, for the occasion.

In contrast the most memorable visual surprise I ever had laid before me was by Lord Eccles, who had commissioned Vanessa Bell to decorate a dessert service with scenes from Virginia Woolf's *Orlando*. He saw that I was served with the 'Elizabethan lady', and my wife with 'the man in the large black hat'. Such is the stage-management of table-laying. It is above all an exercise in the art of looking, and a means whereby even the humblest meal is made unforgettable.

Packets and Labels

ONE ECCENTRIC FRIEND we know reclines in the bath surrounded by empty wine bottles bobbing around him in the water. The labels eventually float off and he scoops them up, carefully dries them and presents them to the Bodleian Library, Oxford, for their ephemera collection.

I suppose it reflects a triumph of the eye over the intellect but an attractive label, box or tin has been responsible for many a foolish purchase. For years I have clung on to some bottles of wine in the cellar not because their content is maturing to some excellence but because the label was designed by Oliver Messel. It is in his customary decorative style, and depicts a central mask with swags of vines looped up either side.

To be seduced by wine-bottle labels cannot be wholly evil. In the case of the remarkable Baron Philippe de Rothschild the result has been an alliance of contents to graphics of quality. Bottles of Mouton Rothschild bear labels by every artist from Vertès to Picasso. I confess that I find it difficult to buy even the most modest plonk unless the label beguiles. They open an eye, however distorted, on to the contents, associating its consumption with a château glimpsed from afar, country folk harvesting grapes, or vine-terraced domains. Other labels embark on optical snobbery and are peppered with crowns and coats of arms. The labelling adopted by the wine societies is invariably lettering only, albeit by the ilk of Reynolds Stone, asserting seriousness of intent and inducing one's downfall.

Packaging in fact gives enormous pleasure, and in no area more in the past decade than in boxes of soap. I always prop up packets of soap around the bathroom just to enjoy the outsides before using the contents. They are beautiful the way they ally the joys of coloured plates from an old botanical book to the demands of the architectural form of a small box. There are delicate sprays of herbs, old roses, flowers of all sorts, leaves and fruit. The designers raid Victorian scraps and eighteenth-century graphics to entrance us into buying rosemary, honeysuckle, tea rose and glycerine, even brown windsor, a variety I always thought was a soup and not a soap.

There is a strongly nostalgic element to it all, as though cleanliness were aligned to a pre-1914 dreamworld. The same technique has been applied to a whole range of foodstuffs which fall into the traditional or home-made category. Jams, marmalades and honeys are placed into delectable octagonal pots with pretty labels and lids. Christmas puddings are dressed up as though from a country house cupboard and not the factory. Biscuits are glossed in the same way and encased in imagery that belies the reality of their manufacture.

Labelling and packaging inevitably work on this 'seeing is believing' principle. We look for suggestions that the product is made by human hand and not machine, that the contents will feed illusions about other eras and that their purchase will place us in a bracket of super taste, elegance and discernment.

It is striking how very patchy is this approach to packaging. To take one instance, the marketing of British cheese on the Continent must be a lost cause on presentation alone. I remember we were dining with the former minister for agriculture Peter Walker, who produced as a finale to the meal one of the earliest Lymeswold cheeses. Delicious cheese, deplorable packaging, we echoed. In any array of cheeses the British always look like lumps of coloured plastic. The foreign ones in contrast are in extraordinary shapes, sit on little straw mats or reside in wooden boxes and bear strange decorative lettering with pictures of country people in exotic traditional dress. Even Stilton looks drab in comparison.

The art of packaging is a strange alliance of good and often bad taste, hard sell and public gullibility. That does not concern me. What I hope is that the designers who have excelled in this art over the last decade realize the transitory delight which their work has brought to everyday things and that they do not merely think we throw their work into the wastepaper basket without casting a lingering look and uttering a sigh of gratitude.

Window Dressing

ONE OF THE GREAT minor arts which has practically been killed off in this country is that of window display. A glance at the Design Centre in the Haymarket will confirm how far we have sunk in this form of presentation.

In London at present only four shops, Harrods, Harvey Nichols, Liberty's and Selfridges, make any attempt at dressing their windows as microcosms of current style. Other stores, like the Army & Navy, have virtually banished display altogether, while Barkers has, for the past few years, been a monument to expensive vulgarity which provides every visitor with regular evidence of our decline in taste and design.

Concern with such a topic may seem trivial, but it is not. Any visitor to a metropolis knows the importance of the contents of shop windows. They, along with advertising in the form of posters, provide the most immediate impression of a country's international awareness of current style and fashion and, more importantly, its own contribution. One of the great pleasures of being in New York is that stroll down Fifth Avenue, above all at Christmas time. The windows of the great department stores are dressed with a breathtaking sense of occasion reflecting the seasons, each tableau a work of art in its own right, telling the potential purchaser of the movement of style by providing, like a fashion magazine, a heightened, even fantastic, vision of it.

In London, that ability has gone, to the detriment of both our commerce and our international image. We had it once, strangely enough in that beleaguered, impoverished, design-reforming era, the 1950s. Janine Janet was the great exponent in Paris, but London had its own genius in Eric Lucking, whose dressing of Liberty's windows was so astounding that, as an art-struck schoolboy, I used to voyage just to stand and stare in wonder at them. And it was all done with bales of fabric and pins without ever wielding scissors. It was a tradition of brilliance kept going by his successor, Roy Gentry. During the same period Simpson's windows were dressed by Natasha Kroll and they too were points of reference on British style. If I could point to an accessible reference as to how far we have travelled from this it would be to the Christmas lights in Regent Street which year by year descend ever deeper into a mire of tasteless kitsch: far better to do away with them altogether.

Ironically, it was the sixties that witnessed the decline of this art. Affluence eroded inventiveness. Perhaps too there was a reaction against the great set pieces in the same way that trade moved from the large stores to the small boutiques in Chelsea and in the Carnaby Street area. In addition there was little public recognition of the huge role that the exponents of this art had played in lifting London as a place of style and fashion.

To me it is a sad loss. It has not been replaced by the Italian approach to window dressing which is based on exquisite sensitivity aligned to supreme calculation. Everything looks thrown into the window of an Italian shop but in a manner which registers all that its contents have to offer in terms of quality and style. A lesson as to how good they are at it is provided by Jermyn and Bond Streets, where the Italians make use of this design principle to the detriment of our own shops, in which the goods are either badly displayed or literally just thrown in.

The English visual sense has never recovered since the Reformation removed images from the eyes and placed them, in the form of words, in the mind. Almost anywhere on the continent there is an instinctive eye for the placing of merchandise, a sense of *joie de vivre* in cascades of fruit, fish or meat. Even the humblest market stall seems to compose itself into a still-life whereas here such ingredients in the main seem dumped. The fish is not arranged on the slab in radiating patterns. The meat and game does not look fit to be painted by Oudry. Even the parsley now is plastic!

This is a sad saga but surely not beyond redemption. Selfridges for one has made the voyage back from the depths. Sainsbury's, for example, could apply its energies to the presentation of food. The role of the display manager should be lifted, recognized and properly paid. Ephemeral it may be, but window dressing embodies an alliance of pleasure-giving to the onlooker with sharp commercial good sense.

Biedermeier Revived

HAPPENING TO WRITE a few words on the historical background to the *Nutcracker* ballet, I found myself looking into the world of the *biedermeier*. The ballet derives, of course, from E. T. A. Hoffmann's story *Nutcracker and the King of Mice* via a French translation by Alexandre Dumas. When the curtain arises on the living-room of the Stahlbaums' house and the famous Christmas party, we are contemplating a scene which is pure *biedermeier*.

As an epoch it lasted roughly from 1815, the year of the Treaty of Vienna, down to 1848, the Year of Revolutions. It was never an English style but one generated in the Austro-Hungarian Empire in the aftermath of the Napoleonic Wars. This was a period when the *ancien régime* was reinstated and the liberal middle classes, denied power, turned in on themselves and created a style of living whose basis was the cultivation of the domestic virtues in the form of all aspects of family life, the home and the garden.

As a style it has long fascinated me ever since I first became aware of the watercolour sketches of these interiors made more widely known by Mario Praz in his *An Illustrated History of Interior Decoration*, first published in 1964. Room after room is filled with a clutter of potted plants, softly upholstered chairs, muslin curtains and sprigged wallpapers. Figures sit writing letters, engaged in games or conversation. One hears the magic of Schubert's music as one's eyes wander over them.

In 1979 I initiated an exhibition on the subject at the Victoria and Albert Museum. It was a complete flop, at least in terms of figures, attracting only 19,000 visitors. Five years on, I suddenly began to notice references to this exhibition and, what is more, witness in decorating magazines a cult of these interiors matched by an increasing interest by the sale rooms in any pieces which come on to the market.

Can one place an interpretation on this *renversement*? I believe that one can. The *biedermeier* era was one in which a class was forced to turn its energies towards not public but private life. In other words, can one postulate a relationship between the cult of a private controllable world as against a public uncontrollable one in which one is assigned no role?

With this hypothesis in mind *biedermeier* came too soon in 1979. It was anticipatory. It is, however, exactly right for the present. A magazine called *The World of Interiors* would, for instance, never have flourished a decade ago: it does now. Any glance at the magazine racks or at the contents of the colour supplements confirms this obsession with the interior of the home and, by extension, with the garden. In the 1960s, in contrast, it was the public face, in the form of clothes.

Today's cult does not, however, spring from any practice of the domestic virtues. The divorce rate alone establishes that. It reflects rather the reassurance of things material, in terms of artefacts old, which evoke reveries of times past, aligned to artefacts new, which advance comfort to new heights. Of course, this also epitomizes other pressures: the spread of the taste for interior design across the social spectrum besides a genuine revival in decoration as such. None the less the socio-political atmosphere must be the supreme key to this birth of a British *biedermeier*.

And the prime exponent must be Laura Ashley. Her migration into wallpapers and fabrics casts her as the popularizer of the style, thanks to a price range which makes it available to vast sections of the modestly affluent in our society. The sources she draws on are significant. It is *au fond* an adaptation for the middle classes of a repertory first evolved by John Fowler in the 1930s for the aristocracy. On to this she has grafted sources as varied as French provincial, 1920s suburban revival, and Victoriana. Its premise is always nostalgia.

It will go down as an odd phenomenon of the recession that the rise in unemployment has gone hand in hand with a parallel rise in expenditure on the private interior. As the exterior world seems to become progressively less safe to walk in, the Englishman's home, even if encircled with burglar alarms, has become even more his castle.

Bathrooms Old and New

A RECENT STATISTIC which caught my eye was the fact that young people are cleaner than ever before. It crossed my mind again when I performed at the speech day of my old grammar school, for one of the most potent memories of that institution was the smell of human bodies, particularly as one changed for the purgatory of the gymnasium or the sports field. It must also have been part of the social divide, for I remember asking Lady Diana Cooper what struck her most at Belvoir Castle when her father, the Duke of Rutland, opened it to the public at the turn of the century. 'The smell', came the reply. Few memories make one more grateful for the spread of the cult of the bathroom and male toiletries.

In great houses there is always an attic or room which contains dusty ranks of washbasins, jugs and soap dishes recalling the days when droves of maids carried water to each bedroom. For centuries the bathroom was a rarity, which is what makes the Duchess of Lauderdale's marble and tiled one in the basement at Ham House an index of her extreme ostentation. It is also what makes the reconstruction at Leeds Castle of the mechanics for a bath in the middle ages, a circular tub lined with fabric and enclosed within a tent, so fascinating. Such arrangements are really not so far away in time. The bathroom as anything other than an exception is only a few generations away.

Indeed of all the changes in room arrangement to occur in this century affecting daily domestic life, the advent and multiplication of bathrooms must be the most significant. Inevitably this began in the great houses but it was not until the 1930s that the ratio of bathrooms to bedrooms began to move into being neck and neck. Plâs Newydd sticks in my mind as an early instance of this comfort which has now spread across the social spectrum, so that a bathroom is a *sine qua non* of ordinary living and to have two or more is by no means unusual.

That is an interesting if dull fact in itself. More fascinating is what gets into that room apart from the plumbing. I vividly recall the first time that I was struck by what is now a commonplace, pictures in the bathroom. About 20 years ago I was doing research on a Tudor artist called Hans Eworth. His earliest work, *A Turk on Horseback*, belonged to Lord Yarborough. Much to my astonishment, on reaching the house, I was ushered into a bathroom to inspect it.

That experience put up a mental marker that a great change was taking place and that henceforth bathrooms could be categorized into those which remained spartan cleansing units and those which had become rooms. The former were all cream paint, scrubbed and polished wood. The only softening features might be a bottle of bath essence, a solitary framed print and a hard wooden chair. The latter, however, responded to the revival of clutter: elaborate wallpapers, banks of pictures, upholstered chairs, serried ranks of delicious smells to pour into the water and piles of books and magazines. From being a room to go into and out of as quickly as possible it had graduated into one in which to live and linger.

What bathrooms most stick in my mind? Christobel, Lady Aberconway's London one must have been the ultimate in *grand luxe* in the pre-war era. It was a half-oval, virtually all marble, but with the straight wall of mirror-glass which completed the geometric form. As Sir Brinsley Ford remarked to me, it made demands on the bather and was definitely only for Venuses. It also made the reconstruction of Tilly Losch's bathroom, which was all mirrors, in the 1930s exhibition at the Hayward Gallery, look positively common.

The others are ones experienced. The first was in what was a vestry of a country house chapel but had been transformed into a tent with the bath in the middle. Wired up for piped Wagner, it is the only time that I have wallowed to the sound of Brünnhilde. The second would be any bathroom in Woburn Abbey. These work on the principle that every guest will forget to bring something and each contains a capacious bowl or basket in which there is everything from toothpaste to an aspirin.

Each in addition has a notice above the bath reminding the bather not to let the tub overflow for it will cause a Henry Holland ceiling to crash down on the heads of the visitors below. I have only seen one other bathroom with a notice to beat that. This time the reminder told the user that on the wall of the room immediately beneath hung the Michelangelo.

Postcards

PICTURE POSTCARDS I count as one of life's great pleasures. I am quite unashamed about rushing to the postcard stand anywhere as soon as I can. It is not views I ever buy, except when I'm abroad, but colour reproductions of works of art or details of them, almost invariably pictures, faces and flowers, animals or tiny bits of landscape.

Purists will be horrified, and I well remember when I was young being lectured on what a distortion they were, how the colours were never true and how infinitely better were the black and white ones. But I remain unconverted, and in any case it is irrelevant when all the year round a card of a watercolour of a chaste *biedermeier* room on the mantlepiece of my office, or a view of an English rococo garden by Thomas Robins in my writing room at home, gives me the continuous pleasure of an object I am only ever likely to see once, providing me with perpetual delight, information and reverie. They make an instant, portable, self-selected art gallery.

Shortly after we married, my wife and I found that we shared the same mascot cards. One was the *Rainbow Portrait of Gloriana* at Hatfield House, the other John Piper's *St Mary le Port, Bristol* in the Tate Gallery. They seemed to confirm an identity of vision. Whenever I visit Hatfield I always stock up on cards of the Rainbow Portrait, a code image for England and hope, and all that's good.

What more appropriate vision to send to John Betjeman on his appointment as Poet Laureate, which we did, and received in turn a page with 'Oh, thank you, thank you, thank you' in gargantuan capitals down it.

For those who came of age in the aftermath of the Second World War, the coloured picture postcard must retain a special magic. Such cards were then virtually a new phenomenon seized upon by the public. For years after, the museums of London touted huge trays of cheap sepia cards from the pre-war era which never seemed to shift. They held no appeal against the thrill of bearing home in colour Rubens's *Chapeau de Paille* or Piero's *Nativity*, two early cult objects. Only now does one yelp with glee over a post office on the remote Welsh borders which throws up racks of 1920s local views in sepia.

On the whole I am a selfish collector. I hardly ever send them from abroad. My handwriting is so unreadable when I do, it is the postmark and the picture which provide the clue as to where I am. No, I prefer to hoard them at home for memory and messages. They encourage concision of expression in correspondence. 'Thank you ... for the marvellous dinner' (still life of food), ... 'for putting us up for the night' (view of a state bed), ... 'having a ghastly time' (monster from Bomarzo or almost anything oriental), '... hope you are better' (Dutch interior with doctor's visit) or '... writing hard at the moment' (evangelist or Shakespeare's tomb).

There are also the 'Go for a walk in ...' variety. This may sound silly but they are a boon for sending to anyone under the weather. Into this category file any kind of complicated meandering view or scene crammed with incident: distant landscapes, vistas and festivals. A page from the *Très Riches Heures*, a large chunk of Gozzoli's *Journey of the Magi* in the Medici Chapel, or *Sir Henry Unton's Memorial Portrait* in the National Portrait Gallery will provide any eye with a journey to muse upon. Counter-Reformation religious art should be avoided for the sick. The wrong image could have fatal results.

So hypnotic do postcards become that I can understand why Ronald Firbank wrote some of his novels on them, although they cannot have been of the picture variety. They surely provide us with endless windows of delight, information and pure sentiment.

If only the artists of the past could know the pleasure they have given by dint of the art postcard. Their creations, in whole or part, take on new life as symbols of travel, friendship and memory. How could Botticelli ever have foreseen that every group, figure and face in his *Primavera* would wing its way around the globe?

Pinned up or propped up, in file and album, far from trivializing the original, they enhance it, extend the wonder and the mystery. How empty my breakfast table would be without them.

Fashion Observed

THE OTHER DAY I went into Herbert Johnson's to buy a new panama hat. One of the assistants asked me the fate of my broad-brimmed fedoras of the late 1960s. 'They are now part of the V & A's dress collection', I replied. 'Oh sir', was the riposte, 'you should have brought them back here and we would have cut the brims down for the later 1970s'. This experience brought to mind a reminiscence of Loelia Lindsay, formerly Duchess of Westminster. Descending the stairs of a great country house for dinner in the aftermath of the First World War she looked down and noticed that none of the Bright Young Things was wearing long white gloves. Quickly she removed the ones that she had on and hid them behind a photograph of Queen 'Ena' of Spain. For me the history of changes in fashion is encapsulated in such trivial anecdotes.

I have only ever seen revolution in dress on a grand scale once. It was in a series of films, taken by an amateur, of clothes worn at Ascot. In the 1947 reel there was an apparition, a lady attired *cap à pied* in the New Look, yards of fabric in defiance of Stafford Cripps. In the 1948 reel every single woman in sight was dressed in this manner, a revolution in appearance as dramatic as the abandonment of paniers two centuries before.

The theory that the silhouette of clothes reflects the growth and decline of the economy seems to me not without some substance. The most famous instance of this is, of course, the collapse of the crinoline in the 1870s coincidental with the beginnings of the great agricultural depression. In our own era the expanding line of the New Look reflected the post-war boom as accurately as the furbelows of the late 1960s mirrored that economic bubble. When it burst in 1974 clothes swiftly caught the mood. Although already anticipated by the designers, men quickly became conformist again, velvet and frills were exiled, long hair and side whiskers were out, and ties, lapels and trousers narrowed to form the thin mean line of the recession.

Histories of fashion always over-simplify. If I were asked the representative garments for the years 1960 to 1985 I would choose one for both sexes, jeans. The recent news that the jeans market is tottering must have the same impact in the end as that which resulted in piles of unsaleable crinoline frames outside Birmingham in the 1870s.

Although jeans began as a classless garment, they were assimilated ultimately into the designer network and voyaged from being the attire of the outré young to becoming the uniform of the middle-aged protester. Flared, frayed, bleached, patched or sewn with brilliants, may this article of clothing now rest in peace. It was the item of dress which *par excellence* epitomized the socialist utopia. That both garment and ideology have worn thin simultaneously is hardly surprising.

When it comes to clothes some of the most singular people are those who decide in which period by deliberation they will defiantly remain. Mrs Reynolds Stone parades still in the quintessence of the New Look, and Mr Bunny Roger remains an early 1950s revived Edwardian dandy. He can still be spotted strolling along Piccadilly in curled bowler, waisted jacket, narrow trousers, a furled umbrella and a carnation in his buttonhole. Lord Stockton must be the last true Edwardian, slightly dandified but with a shambling quality to his appearance that evokes a cartoon by Ape for *Vanity Fair*. The

Bloomsbury spirit lives on in Lady (Charlotte) Bonham Carter in her long skirts and blouses over which she pins an arrangement of shawls that place her as a direct descendant of Dorelia and Augustus John's gypsies.

The recent fashion for wearing old clothes could only ever have emerged with the advent of expendability in the 1960s. Prior to that clothes had to last. That plus the mania for dressing up led to the discovery of the joys of old clothes. I remember seeing Mariga Guinness in the late 1960s appearing each night with a different 1870s dress, a whimsical trait made the stranger because of the absence of the same period's undergarments. In fact the best sort of old clothes are those found in the back halls and cloakrooms of country houses; rows of boots and shoes, heaps of Norfolk and hacking jackets in tweed, explosions of hats from felt to straw for all weathers. The smell and the patina of them are precious, for there they remain for each generation to rifle through to plod over moor and park land.

One of the advantages of age is the firm adoption of an immutable look. Lady Diana Cooper, like the late Queen Mary, is now a monument to this. Indomitable in her nineties, she now makes all her public appearances wearing the same black feathered hat. When, some years back, I quizzed her as to its source, she replied, 'Someone left it to me.' That too ranks high amongst my anecdotes mirroring the passage of fashion.

'ALL THINGS BRIGHT AND BEAUTIFUL...'

Trees

Cats

Flowers

Fruit

Garden Visions

Snow

Trees

A CEDAR of Lebanon guards our house. I look out on it as I write. It is supposed to have been planted in 1815 and acts as a mnemonic for the date of the battle of Waterloo; it is also the first tree that I ever really got to know well. It has been a good friend and a noble teacher because I have been frantically looking at and planting trees ever since.

It is an even better inspiration to be exposed to the enthusiasms of a genuine 'tree man'. The late Sir Richard Cotterell, a peppery soul and guardian of a mighty Repton landscape, was such. His eye and mind were all trees. Once he walked me round his creation, Queen's Wood, just outside Hereford, planted to commemorate the coronation. We paused at each tree or group of trees, considered its form and shape, when it was planted, and its rate of growth. There was almost a solemnity about our stately progress.

With another 'tree man', Lawrence Banks, one swoops from one trunk to the next at Hergist Croft, exclaiming over its texture and colour with a fervour of aesthetic appreciation more generally applied to an antique textile. It is always exciting to be in touch with a way of looking at things which most of us bypass. For most ordinary mortals, trees are just things that happen to be there. I would quite like one day to go on a great trees of Britain tour in the same way as we visit our cathedrals or country houses. I for one have already begun to compile a personal anthology of favourites.

I would have to begin with the ancient oaks of England, and none for me can surpass those in the royal chase at Hatfield. I was once taken to see them by the late Dowager Marchioness of Salisbury in a hair-raising cross-field expedition to trace the eighteenth-century road that still remains there, a monument to times past when roads actually went round trees. There they were, vast gnarled specimens that must have witnessed many a royal hunting party, and beneath one of which the young Elizabeth I was sitting on the November day that the news came from London of her sister's death.

That, sadly, is now only a stump, so I would have to include another royal tree, the Boscobel oak, or rather its descendant. That still flourishes, although I have only seen it across the fields from the mount in the garden. The original perished as a result of the onslaught of souvenir hunters avid for twigs and whole branches. I would also have to include the vast evergreen or holm oak at Westbury-upon-Severn, whose mighty branches are supported from below by props. And the elms of Worcestershire would also have figured but, alas, are no more part of the elegiac pattern of Elgar's landscape.

The only fruit trees that stick in my mind are those trained into extraordinary shapes. There is a spectacular group at Powis Castle, first glimpsed from above. They have been tied and trained into orderly domes as exact as though they had been composed with the sweep of a compass arc. At Barnsley House, Gloucestershire, the new *potager* has, as centre points of the vegetable beds, apple trees trained as crowns. And there is the marvellous avenue of venerable espaliered apple trees that leads away from Cranborne Manor towards great gates and the beyond.

And that brings me to avenues. The majestic sweep of sweet chestnuts down the hill away from Croft Castle would come high on my list. So would the pleached lime avenue at Sissinghurst, Kent. I would add to this the Lombardy poplar avenue planted by the late Duke of Wellington in the house he lived in near Stratfield Saye in Hampshire, arranged in a steep false perspective up towards the skyline and thus seeming to stretch into infinity.

Does the stilt hedge of hornbeam at Hidcote, Gloucestershire, count? I hope so, as I have a personal penchant for the architectural treatment of trees which must be anathema to the pure 'tree man'. John Fowler copied this effect for his Gothic lodge in his minute masterpiece of a garden at Odiham, which would also have to be included. He once taught me how to get mistletoe to grow in the boughs of fruit trees, but I have never been able to achieve it.

But perhaps my favourite single tree is one just outside Stow-on-the-Wold, by which I have driven times without number. It is a variety of *acer palmatum*, a small tree with a crown of leaves which unfurl in the spring, blush pink streaked with the palest green. Perfect in form, it arises at the side of an entrance to a great house directly opposite the lodge. Every spring one waits for the magic moment when this astonishing beacon blazes once more. I always feel grateful to whoever planted it for siting this rare and exotic tree where everyone who drives along the road from Tewkesbury to Burford over the Cotswolds can savour its glory.

Cats

IT IS A FACT that animals, if one has them, dominate one's life. I never sought the two cats that determine mine. They arrived from nowhere over the fields and progressively took us over, in the end graciously allowing us to be their guests in a house now entirely arranged for them with myriad saucers and plates, boxes and bowers and holes cut in practically everything to facilitate their passage. The surrender is total.

The large, long-haired cat with doleful green eyes is called the Reverend Wenceslas Muff because, when reclining, he resembles exactly Hollar's engraving of a muff of the kind a lady would have carried in Caroline England. 'Wenceslas' after the artist and his clerical bands he owes to his colour. The Lady Torte de Shell, of the white, black and ginger fur, speaks for itself.

Cats deserve interesting names and I've no time for anything called Ginger or Blackie. It's like calling a rose Shandy or Rita. Cecil Beaton's cat was called Timothy White, after the chemist's I assume, a huge white creature that I remember arriving plonk on my bed in the middle of the night. John Schlesinger has a cat called Placido because it came through the front door at the time he was staging his production of *The Tales of Hoffman*, starring Placido Domingo.

The local farmer's wife oddly commemorated the recent royal birth by naming three farmyard cats Charles, Diana and William. One Renaissance scholar, I recall, had a cat named after the fifteenth-century Neo-Platonic philosopher Marsiglio

Ficino. The late Dame Frances Yates, who was the nearest thing to Ficino come round again, was adopted in old age by a creature she called, somewhat unimaginatively, Pussy. In her last years Pussy dominated her existence. She used to plan her exits from her house at Claygate so that he wouldn't notice. Out this formidable lady would rush from the entrance opposite to the one to which she had lured the cat, only to find that it had torn its way round to the other side of the house and would be sitting looking up at her.

A. L. Rowse is the only person I know who used to ring up one of his cats from the United States. They apparently had lively interchanges. Although the telephone receiver has been held close to both our animals I have never been able to achieve this degree of communication. Ours seem to attract, however, quite an international correspondence fom artists, scholars and members of the aristocracy, besides lavish gifts of toy birds and mice stuffed with catnip.

E. Box, the painter, is a favourite correspondent and she has painted the Lady Torte de Shell's portrait on the lid of a box, setting her amidst foliage and beneath a mysterious moon. The cats that she paints stare out from her canvases with human eyes. They roam through long grass, sit by the dozen in trees or perch on windowsills, but always with eyes that look out. Hardly surprising really, as she doesn't like cats, having a dog called Fred with a literary correspondent in Lesley Blanch, who sends him skipping ropes and chocolate cigarettes.

E. Box's pictures quickly find their way onto greetings cards. There is a minor industry here, serried ranks of cat cards bearing everything from Stubbs's white kitten on a velvet cushion to today's caricature cards. As an animal, the cat on the whole has been pretty unfashionable, certainly not an attribute of the establishment classes like the dog, as the history of portraiture abundantly tells. The present cat cult, I suppose, serpentines its way down via Grandville to Edward Lear, but my earliest memory of the cat as hero is Orlando, the marmalade cat, during the postwar period. Orlando has had a mighty progeny since, down to Nicola Bayley's *The Patchwork Cat*. Both, incidentally, epitomize the best in children's book illustration.

A more prolific exponent of the present cat cult is the artist Martin Leman, who paints nothing but cats. A genuine primitive, he asks us to contemplate the cat as icon. He reduces them to mounds of fur brooding on a brick wall or by the seashore, or arising from a bed of formalized flowers.

What will the historian of the twentieth century make of this vast outpouring in worship of the cat? Not much, I would have thought; not more than the subjects that have evoked it in such beguiling plenitude. In this we are victims of ourselves and not of our animals.

Flowers

TWO EVENTS in a matter of weeks called to mind the pleasure of summer flowers. One was Peter Wilson's memorial service at St George's, Hanover Square, where the altar was flanked by arrangements fifteen feet high, incorporating huge lilies, and which ranked as masterpieces in their own right as much as any of those auctioned off during his life. The second was strolling through the court of a Cambridge college being dressed for a May Ball, and seeing pampas grass and Technicolor blooms arranged to rape Wren's architecture. Strange, one thought, that such intrinsically beautiful things should be able simultaneously to decorate or desecrate according into whose hands they fall.

In June we come to those lush months in which even the most fervent of gardeners will actually allow flowers to be cut for the house because no one will notice that they have gone. We in fact enjoy a luxury of flowers unknown to many countries. So precious are they in Sweden, for example, that it is by no means regarded as stingy to arrive and present just one bloom. But we, with our lingering cult of the herbaceous border and of the rose, have them in abundance – not that one would know it from the average florist's shop.

Miss Jean Brodie, on being presented with a bunch of flowers by her pupils, paused and remarked: 'Chrysanthemums, such serviceable flowers.' They must have been that terrifying phenomenon known as 'All-the-year-round chrysanthemums', a variety which ought to be firmly cemented into the floor of Hades along with carnations with four-feet stems and roses that remain obdurately in bud. On the whole the high-street florist has become the purveyor of floral kitsch, inevitable when even nature has to be standardized, with flower varieties reduced to as few as possible, all grown to have exactly the same size, height and appearance.

In this debasement of the flower, for such it is, they are more than ably assisted by a movement in the various flower-arranging societies. This promotes the creation of compositions, labelled with subjects reminiscent of a Victorian Royal Academy exhibition, into which swags of fabric, old bits of wood, china figurines and other pieces of tat are introduced to evoke 'Sunrise' or 'Marie Antoinette'. Equally baleful has been the influence of abstract art. Both movements are guilty of trying to turn flowers into something that they are not.

The only professional florist whose work can always be categorized as art is Kenneth Turner. I was first aware of it at a reception at the National Portrait Gallery for Annigoni's second portrait of the Queen. For this he made voluptuous garlands in the Edwardian manner cascading twenty feet down the wall on either side of Lavery's silvery vision of George V and his family. Later he embellished an exhibition of beauties through the ages, the floor of which he carpeted with beech leaves. This had an unfortunate effect on hay-fever sufferers, some of whom were carried out feet first. He, together with a handful of the better London shops, still maintains what can only be described as the grand tradition.

That also had and still has its amateur exponents. Cecil Beaton was a genius with flowers. Reddish House was filled with them, vases everywhere, in the spring clear glass into which bundles of daffodils were thrown (they should never be arranged), succeeded by huge branches of white and purple lilac and then an unending season of roses arranged *à la Fantin*

Latour. I always recall him drawling: 'Remember, Roy, white flowers are the only chic ones.' The other person with a similar flair was the late Lord Plunket, who orchestrated the decor for great occasions in the royal palaces, huge explosions of foliage and blossoms soaring up to the ceiling of Windsor Castle or Buckingham Palace.

The moral of this tale is that flowers either have to be very grand or very simple. In the local market there is still the joy of the humble bouquet of cottage-garden flowers: violets and primroses in the spring, old roses and pinks in the summer. They retain a quite unconscious sense of style because those who put them together also grew them. Even the tiniest bunch is their garden in microcosm.

I know that it is fashionable these days to have no flowers at one's funeral, and viewing the average tasteless pile-up the decision is hardly a surprising one, even if the motive is ostensibly charitable. I, however, would prefer to go to my grave with just one of those nosegays atop me than an acre of 'All-the-year-round chrysanthemum' crosses.

Fruit

Now is the orchard laden. Just the sight of a fruit tree in the golden autumn sun with its branches gently bending beneath its burden leaves one with both an aesthetic and culinary glow. For fruit is beautiful both on and off the tree. Indeed its whole cycle from spring blossom to delectable consumption is a delight. It is part of both landscape and garden and, separated from the branch, it is still-life.

The other week we went to see a friend's ancient apple tunnel. By ancient, in terms of fruit trees, it cannot have been older than a century. It was the remnants of a bold concept, a passage encircling the path around a huge walled kitchen garden. To be embowered within an architecture of old gnarled trunks and branches hung with fruit is an experience touching most of the senses. And among those trees, lost varieties had been discovered.

In an age of the Golden Delicious, the spur to seek out and plant old varieties of fruit tree is irresistible. At Westbury-upon-Severn the National Trust has restored and replanted the late seventeenth-century garden in just such a way. The garden is in the Dutch manner, with an elegant summer house at the head of a long rectangular canal. But we always wander along the walls studying the old fruit trees, each one neatly labelled and dated: Royal Russett (1597) and Colville Blanc d'Hiver (1660) apples, Catillac (1665) and Forelle (1670) pears and D'Agen (before 1600) plums. It is a planting which indicates that the French have been more successful at keeping their older varieties alive than we have.

It reminds one too that a principal source for fruit trees in the past, in addition to the Low Countries, was France. They were imported for the palaces of Henry VIII and shiploads came from Normandy under the aegis of John Tradescant for the planting of Hatfield in the Jacobean period. And it was from there that Archbishop Laud's friend Lord Scudamore brought the cider apples of Herefordshire which he cultivated at Holme Lacy during the Commonwealth. One sees their lineal descendants to this day in the huge cider orchards dotted across the county.

The earliest tree in our orchard is a Devonshire Quarrenden, a small bright red dessert apple which ripens early and is first referred to in 1685. I would dearly love a Pearmain, our oldest apple, recorded in 1204 and apparently still alive in the 1940s. From the late seventeenth century, apples skip a century or more down to Blenheim Orange (1818), Orléans Reinette (1776) and Braddicks Nonpareil (1800). And then follows the Victorian progeny that always used to leave me wondering above all as to who was the Rev. W. Wilks.

Apples seem to have a romance virtually denied to our other fruits, although only the English could transform the plum Reine Claude, named in honour of François I's queen, into Green Gage, after Sir William Gage of Hengrave Hall. One would think that there would be an abundance of anecdote also on our English quinces, but no. Every time one catches their perfume, however, one understands exactly why they were placed for fragrance in the linen cupboards of Pepys's day.

In our age we tend to put fruit trees in a separate area of even the smallest garden but in earlier times orchard and pleasure garden were almost interchangeable, the trees being planted to form geometric patterns and walks. Like topiary, they can give a garden structure when espaliered and sculpture when trained as crowns, domes and pyramids. Alas, what art we have lost.

On the whole we are in retreat. The pressure is to fewer and fewer varieties and this is matched by an equally banal and unimaginative use of them. The appearance of an apple tunnel at the Chelsea Flower Show in 1984 may signal a turn of the tide. Let us remember that our forefathers maintained orangeries, and now I can think of very few still operable. That at Kensington Palace has been used by the Prime Minister to receive visiting EEC leaders. Three centuries ago it would have housed orange and lemon trees in vast tubs awaiting the summer sun for them to be wheeled out and dotted about the parterres. How sad that they are there no longer.

Garden Visions

JUST BEFORE Christmas the bowls of hyacinths so carefully nurtured in the dark by my wife are brought out to scent the drawing room and breakfast table during the festive season. And then, in the New Year, the postman delivers envelopes and little parcels full of those symbols of the seasons to come, packets of seeds.

I always marvel at the pleasure that nursery catalogues and pictorial seed packets bring. They feed the inner world of illusion, going back to childhood when one was presented with Rainbow or Cottage Garden Mix. One stared at the magic vision with its obligatory picturesque cottage arising amidst an explosion of hollyhocks, marigolds, nemesia and sweet-smelling stocks. For a moment one believed that if its contents were scattered on the tiny patch of earth assigned one, three months later one would be strolling through the picture. Alas, it never happened, but surely the whole point of those packets lay in the dream and not the reality.

All purveyors of plants and seeds play on that inner Arcady. I don't in the least resent it and unashamedly buy packets of seeds by the picture on the outside regardless of the practicality as to whether the contents will grow or not. It is rather like purchasing wine by the beauty of the label, another vice. The vegetables in the pictures are always beautiful and of lush proportions. And they are always growing in neat tended rows with never a slug in sight. Having a romantic approach, even to the vegetable garden, it is depressing to find the seed order reduced to numbers and plain packets with typed labels.

The Dowager Lady Radnor once remarked to me: 'Remember, it is very vulgar to buy plants.' I regret to say that although the garden is full of donations from the great houses, I cannot resist that vulgarity. The nursery catalogues cleverly arrive at the dead-end of autumn and provide instant reverie; even those without colour plates embark on a particular genre of beguiling prose. Catalogues of roses, for example, leave me mesmerized: 'Silky, pale yellow, full-petalled flower of old-fashioned formation', 'Flowers of the darkest rich velvet crimson which do not fade', 'Peach pink with a silvery reverse'. Instantly one imagines them nodding in profusion and scenting the air of one's own garden.

Horticultural shows depend on the same pyschological principle. They present and excite the onlooker with the unattainable. The seasons are visibly vanquished as tulips, roses and poppies are all seen simultaneously at their apogee. Every flower and fruit is of the best, all there to be ordered for delivery. Engulfed by such a phantasmagoria, resentment only enters in with unavailability. Well do I remember my wrath after the excitement of seeing newly-bred tulips of the seventeenth-century kind flaunted in a huge tulip vase, to be told that there were none for sale. I felt like Lady Bracknell denied her delicious cucumber sandwiches.

Books on gardens, of which we are in the middle of a boom, work towards the same end. The texts are secondary, the pictures everything. In this instance pictures of gardens before the age of photography purvey no sense of reality. They remain wholly archaeological. It is those volumes produced before the First World War that become the point of reference for aspirations and none more so than Avray Tipping's three-volume *Gardens Old and New*.

These folios with their highly evocative photographs by

Charles Latham record the gardens of the great houses of Edwardian England before the deluge and thereby exert a potent spell. They provide images to linger and dream over as one glimpses a lady with a parasol strolling under a rose pergola, a scrolled ironwork gate flung wide to a vista beyond, or a parterre of clipped box and yew.

Like the brightly coloured picture on the Cottage Garden Mix they swing open a window into an Arcadia that is peculiarly English. Half the delight of gardening stems from this constant voyage of the imagination and nothing encapsulates better both its joys and its inescapable poignancy.

The garden ideal is part of the English vision and never more strongly than at present. In this it touches a vital nerve, for even the seed packet is a humble reflection of the role of the garden in our national mythology, re-echoing the eternal birth and rebirth of the realm itself.

Snow

A FLURRY of snow threw a thin mantle of white over the branches of the trees the other day. Two lines come to mind whenever I see it. One is by Christina Rossetti in her carol 'In the bleak mid-winter', with its words 'snow on snow, snow on snow'; the other occurs in Christopher Fry's play *The Dark is Light Enough*, when someone refers to the snow outside falling 'soft and white as a bishop's hand in blessing'.

As romance and spectacle, snow made a late debut. On the whole it figures as just bad weather, a harbinger of misery, cold and inconvenience, certainly not as something to enjoy, let alone make the subject of works of art. I always think of the seventeenth and nineteenth centuries as snow centuries, whereas it doesn't figure in my vision of either the eighteenth or the twentieth. This is probably the result of weather history, for the former two were marked by intensely cold winters, ones which even saw the Thames frozen over. Once I actually met someone who remembered, as a child in the 1880s, when that last happened.

Can anything in fact have been more picturesque than those Frost Fairs held in Pepys's day when shops and booths sprang up across the ice-bound river? Coaches and sledges plied their way along this highway and Evelyn describes 'sheds, sliding with skates, or bull-baiting, horse and coach races, puppet-shows and interludes, cooks, tippling and other lewd places; so that it seemed to be a bacchanalian triumph or carnival on water ...'

Shortly after, in 1691, came the first major snow and ice scene on stage, in Purcell's *King Arthur*. It had nothing to do with the main plot and includes the really terrible couplet penned by Dryden for Cupid to utter: 'In spight of Cold weather, I've brought ye together'. The snow in our pantomime transformation scenes is literally a lineal descendant of this 'Prospect of Ice and Snow'.

Strangely for a country which has a great tradition of landscape art, snow and ice figure remarkably little. For this we have to turn to the minor masters of Holland's golden age. Those endless paintings by Avercamp and others recording the joys of winter provide just the type of strip-serial approach made for a meandering eye bent on incident. Ladies muffled up seated in sledges drawn by horses across the iced-over canals, gentlemen in tall hats and baggy trousers playing golf, and skaters of all sorts everywhere. Three centuries later they have provided the manufacturers of Christmas cards with a veritable hoard of delectable images.

Sledges remain a very un-English mode of transport. Although there are some fetching prints of an ermine-clad Queen Victoria being propelled in one by the Prince Consort, we have nothing to rival the bizarre vehicle of mad Ludwig of Bavaria, let alone the imperial sledges in the Kremlin. The most amazing must be the one made for Catherine the Great, literally a rococo room, painted and gilded all over and capable of bearing at least a dozen people. Lit from within and drawn by teams of horses, it must have looked like some gigantic lantern floating through the darkness as it bore the empress from St Petersburg to Moscow.

The passion for snow is not always a good-taste one. It is responsible for those plastic domes containing an object which, when shaken, can be contemplated in a mini snowstorm. A friend, as a student, was once commissioned to purchase the cheapest instance of bad design that he could find. It was one of these objects, in the form of a television set with a madonna and child inside permanently surrounded by swirling snowflakes.

Such lapses are the inevitable result of a stream of thought that romaticizes snow. It is canonized above all in the Christmas card whose iconography remains *au fond* fixed in the bad weather conditions of late Victorian England. Ladies in vast crinolines trudge to church through mountains of snow, carol singers clutching lanterns chorus away as it engulfs them, while the poor starved robin perches forever on a snow-laden bough. And snow surely must account for the popularity of what otherwise would make a very odd addition to the Anglican calendar, St Wenceslas. He would have sunk without trace years ago if he had undertaken his mission in conditions any other than of snow 'deep and crisp and even'.

Times and tides
W
E
MK

For Sale

The Heritage

Instant Antiquity

Romance and Revivalism

Memorial Services

The Demise of Domestics

Birthdays

St George's Day

Homage to the Heralds

Brains and the British

For Sale

I HOPE that I am not alone in finding advertisements for houses hypnotic reading matter. It is a sad confession that much of the appeal of that delectable old war-horse *Country Life* springs from the voyage of the mind and the imagination triggered off by the property pages. Property in the glossies is superior property and that is part of the attraction. Financial constraints are put aside and one reframes one's existence in a Victorian rectory in Staffordshire, a castle in Sutherland or a Georgian terrace house in Bath. Busily one tots up the living rooms and bedrooms – assigning them to occupants *en passant* – the service areas and the extent of the garden, arranging oneself and one's artefacts into them.

The vocabulary used is so limited that one feels anyone working in an estate agent's must be either illiterate or part of some plot to kill off the English language: 'excellent', 'superb', 'exclusive', 'impressive', 'elegant', 'charming'. The word 'luxury' has certainly shed its biblical overtones indicative of untold decadent excess. I remain haunted by the notion that there must exist, hidden away somewhere, a glossary that agents use which actually defines what is meant by 'quiet', 'secluded', 'superb', 'gracious', 'lovely', 'outstanding', 'well-appointed' and 'original'.

There are four distinct phases in looking at these advertisements. The earliest is that of youth, merely day-dreaming; the next is that of the reality of the search; the third is one of greed, gloating over what is hopefully a rising investment, a conclusion to be sustained by looking for similar properties and seeing what they cost; finally, there comes the moment of unloading, when one comes face to face with one's own dwelling pinned up in an estate agent's window or printed in a newspaper or magazine.

Those in the business know how pathetically gullible we all are, for we are bombarded with endless new glossy magazines which are given away, paid for entirely by the advertising of property. These publications in the main seem to record presences at parties, the inevitable guides to food and drink, a profile of a personality, and, above all, column inches on each area of London and its current rating in the investment stakes. They are deeply off-putting, and the paper on which they are printed invariably smells.

It is striking, however, that no photograph actually fully conveys the intangible atmosphere of a home. Everyone who has hunted for a house or flat knows that. The reality is always quite different. It can be as elementary as the fact that if the camera's lens had moved either a fraction to the left or right, it would have taken in the gas filling station or the silage tower. More inexplicable is that feeling of arriving to view a place and knowing that it is not even worth getting out of the car. Sometimes that gut reaction only happens within, when one is overpowered by a sudden sense of alienation, as though the walls exuded a sinister rejection.

That aura of good or ill, happiness or gloom, joy or melancholy, emanates from encounters with even the humblest of dwellings. It is quite unnerving. Ghosts, I suppose. Ghosts of another sort can be compiled going around empty houses where there is always just enough left of the previous occupants to piece together their existence. Did they really live in such squalor? Whatever went on in that bathroom painted black? And I don't like to think what happened in the games room! Simultaneously projecting one's own life onto the building, the mind recreates the one that has gone.

At no time in our history can there have been such an acreage of paper devoted to the change in ownership of domestic residences. What a mine of social history they present: architecture, interiors, an index to what was thought of as modern or new in terms of facilities and comforts. How I would love to have turned over the imaginary pages of advertisements from the Tudor or Stuart period. Whereas we dwell on the virtues of central heating or the addition of a swimming pool, they would have highlighted such novelties as glazed windows, a garden or, rarer still, a bathroom. And the language of sale would have been that of the Authorized Version: 'goodly', 'fair', 'majestic', 'comely' and 'stately'.

The Heritage

THE WORD heritage is beginning to make me shudder. I therefore had more than a little sympathy with Marghanita Laski, who was complaining along the same lines the other day in a letter to *The Times*. Significantly for her it evoked a great deal of merchandise in the worst taste. Heritage was essentially a 1970s cult which has now spread down the social scale.

We all know the heritage cast, the familiar names from the great houses, the odd museum director or two, the lobby of MPs: everyone from Lord Montague to Hugh Leggatt, from Countess Spencer to myself. We have all been at it for years. I remember speaking on the stage of the Lyceum Theatre with Lady Spencer in 1974 on the subject of heritage and both of us have never looked back since. And the subjects are always the same, with the same old vocabulary and phrases: 'Owners and visitors', 'Taxation and the country house', 'Can (whatever it is) survive/be saved for the nation?', and so on, a mixture often of self-congratulation and breast-beating. In 1974 we had the year of the country house, in 1975 European Architectural Heritage Year, in 1979 the Year of the Garden and in 1982 Maritime England. It goes on and on. One day we are going to run out of labels for a particular year.

In my blackest moods I sometimes think that this country's addiction to heritage is eroding its will to go on. It is an industry kept going by a hundred and one societies from the National Trust onwards and hysteria about the heritage is a permanent media feature. The worship of the past and what it created has been taken to an extreme unknown to any previous century. This is undeniable. It is a total distortion of what the word heritage actually means, 'that which has been or may be inherited', which embraces not only the past but also the present. It is high time that everyone dwelt on that fact. It includes now, today, the material culture of the present. We do not want tourists only to come to see our historic heritage. We want them also to come to see a contemporary one in terms of new buildings, new works of art, new environments, new artefacts down to the humblest domestic articles, all integrated together as a single unfolding statement. On the whole tourists cannot buy our past heritage but they can buy our present one. The maintenance of our past heritage depends on creating a present one and marketing it successfully in the world.

So many people concerned with the historic heritage have a total inability to come to terms with the reality of the century in which they live. Nothing is deader than dead heritage and there is too much dead heritage around. The past has swallowed us up. Tourists to Britain must register this. Everywhere they look, historic heritage seems to equal contemporary fossilization.

I used to recoil at the introduction of new things into historic environments. I now realize it was because they were the *wrong* new things, not that they were new. Enormous sums are consumed in restoring and maintaining the *status quo* to the point of the past denying us a future. To my mind the balance has gone wrong. You see it in so many country houses. Apart from a superficial overlay of photographs and magazines, the clock stopped in 1914. There is the odd exception but one has to think hard.

Everyone concerned with Britain's historic heritage also has a duty to its present one. All the applause in this world goes to saving something from the past and restoring it. What about an award to a private owner or institution which commissions and adds new works of art and craftsmanship to an existing historic environment? We desperately need to reestablish the marriage of past and present as it always was. We need to see a new tapestry in the drawing room, new silver alongside the old in the dining room, new furniture, fabrics, wallpapers, carpets, new pictures and prints everywhere taking their place with the old and not rejected or allocated to a compound. Where would any country house owner be without a twentieth-century kitchen? But I have never known an owner commission one from a contemporary designer.

Unless changes and additions are made, by the next century all that visitors will see in any historic environment is a mummified, dead world denying continuity and change. Heritage is a sacred trust. It is what is presented to visitors from abroad as the essence and glory of this country. If that can only be given in terms of yesterday there is little hope of a tomorrow.

Instant Antiquity

Every time the milk goes sour I rush into the garden and pour it over a phoney urn or obelisk to encourage the growth of moss and lichen and thus give the object the patina of age. One of the more curious phenomena of our era is this cult of antiquing artefacts, of artificially inducing the hand of Time. It is not one we apply to everything; for instance, a mighty industry is sustained to achieve exactly the opposite effect in the case of the female face.

Reproduction furniture illustrates the point well. The really best sort has scratches and stains added to the surfaces and a mysterious person known as an artificial woodwormer pelts the pieces with shot, thus leaving phoney woodworm holes everywhere. Italy is the country where the manufacture of items conceived as old when new is a major industry. Any visitor to Florence is familiar with the acres of carved baroque gilt dulled down by a liberal application of a dirt mix.

Even pottery is wiped over to achieve the same effect. Recently I noticed a few deliberate chips. These tricks must be as old as tourism itself, for everyone from the north went south to bring back something old. These modern souvenirs are lineal descendants of the fake antique sculpture produced for those on the Grand Tour.

Instant antiquity by means of deliberate damage and dirt thus has a long history. In the case of gardens it stems from the cult of ruins and the Renaissance desire to make the garden a place in which to evoke dreams of the vanished glories of Greece and Rome. On to this, in England, we can add the romantic obsession with Gothic ruins, be they real or phoney, in the eighteenth century. Tudor and Stuart gardens, in contrast, were monuments to glorious Technicolor as, each year, wooden posts bearing heraldic animals were gaudily painted and gilded. We have never returned to this way of looking at objects in a garden, instead pouring on the liquid manure and whatever else will induce age quickly.

On the whole we don't have the same criterion for our clothes. No one hastens a suit to bagginess and fraying at the cuffs to score an effect. That is permissible to a degree only with country clothes, which should never look new, especially those for work in the garden. Valerie Finnis, Lady Scott, a great gardener, had a hoard of old garden clothes so stiff with mud they almost stood up on their own.

When it comes to interiors our attitudes enter a complex of contradictions which would fill a volume. They are summed up, however, by an exchange between my wife and the chatelaine of a large country house. The latter had rushed across a room and surprisingly apologized for her curtains, to which the reply came: 'You have waited fifty years for these to look so beautiful.' They were of green velvet with borders and great tassels mottled by decades of fading by the sun which, according to one's eye and viewpoint, either made them a work of infinite subtlety or just tattered old fabric that ought to be replaced.

Whether a particular thing ought to appear old or new, let alone whether it should be helped to appear venerable, affects everything we look at. On the whole we never think about it but it is a subject which can cause deep divides and irrational conflicts. The case for cleaning or not cleaning pictures or buildings, for example, can be argued on scientific and historical grounds but the fundamental reaction depends entirely on two subjective rival ways of looking at the world around us. It is the areas of the battleground which are curious, for neither side would expect a car or a piece of kitchen equipment to look old or grubby.

The cult of the hand of Time was born of the discovery of a sense of the historic past which, in terms of human history, is a recent development. No one until that happened would have made head or tail of Crabbe's lines 'For time hath soften'd what was harsh when new, And the stains are all of sober hue.' The consequences arising from this particular concept have bedevilled us ever since.

Romance and Revivalism

ONE OF MY earliest memories of theatre-going in the post-war era was Ivor Novello's *King's Rhapsody* in 1947. Set in some mythical Balkan kingdom, it told the story of a royal marriage, a tale leading to revolution, political perfidy and exile as the audience was swept at breakneck speed from court ball to peasant merrymaking. It ended inevitably with Ivor kneeling clutching a rose before an altar in a gloomy cathedral in the aftermath of his son's coronation. The curtain descended as we choked back the tears.

I must confess that I loved it. Over the way at Drury Lane *Oklahoma* thundered out its raucous choruses as the antithesis to what seemed to many the dying fall of an effete, insular, romantic tradition that 1939 should have killed off completely. But did it?

The exponents of the modernist movement would rise from their graves if they knew that British romanticism is alive and kicking. Readers of *The Times* must have stopped in their tracks recently when Clive Aslet reproduced pictures of Quinlan Terry's nymphaeum and Temple of Venus at West Wycombe, examples of romantic follies of a type that were being built all over the place in the 1790s. Is this a revival of the between-the-wars romance that gave us Raymond Erith's neo-Georgian architecture, the Sitwells' cult of the rococo, Beaton's portraits of the Queen Mother in the manner of Winterhalter, or the caprices of Rex Whistler? Or did it never expire?

The latter is in fact true, for ever since the first Elizabethans built mock medieval castles the British have never lost their penchant for the dream world of other ages. The products of this passion are naturally never referred to by the high priests of the modernist movement, who would see their mere existence as an admission of defeat. At the most they would dismiss its creations as junk, trivia, an irrelevance in a world of skyscrapers and motorways. In this I believe that they will be proved wrong. And in any case the two are not mutually exclusive.

Who are the custodians of the British romantic tradition? Of the arts, ballet must rank as a prime purveyor. Although both Ashton and MacMillan can work within a strictly contemporary idiom, their contribution represents a single chain linking the romanticism of the 1920s and '30s with today. Ashton's *Enigma Variations* (1968) and *A Month in the Country* (1976) can be regarded as significant moments in the reemergence of a tradition which had gone underground in the 1950s and '60s. MacMillan's three fine ballets *Anastasia*, *Manon* and *Mayerling* take the story with vigour into the 1980s, and the young choreographer Michael Corder looks like continuing it into the next century.

Ballet contrasts sharply with straight theatre, where the romantic tradition of acting and production, epitomized above all by Gielgud, has been expunged. One sees no flickers of a comeback here, although I would predict success for the first producer who dared tackle Shakespeare in this way again.

In painting, John Piper must rank as the key link figure. The exhibition at the Tate Gallery to celebrate his eightieth birthday focused our attention on his huge contribution to the romantic tradition in his visions of houses, churches and gardens. Artists within the academic tradition of a John Ward or a Claude Harrison belong to this stream and, as we move to the coming generation, the work of the Mynott brothers tells us that there is no lack of talented successors. And in the field of illustration Nicola Bayley is pure romance.

When we turn to interior decoration, John Fowler is the crucial bridge that takes the romantic style through to today in the work of those he influenced and trained, such as David Mlinaric and Peter Hood. Laura Ashley's recent departure in the presentation of her fabrics, from cottage curtains to country house swags and festoons, pinpoints the sudden spread of such romantic decoration across a wider social spectrum, attracting those who in the 1960s would have adopted Habitat modern. And the new magazine *The World of Interiors* nourishes this vision, emphasized by a stable of photographers, such as Fritz von der Schulenburg or John Vere Brown, skilled in soft focus, mist and haze.

I could elaborate on the theme but how can I conclude? All of this is a question of emphasis and selectivity. At the moment the 'official' history of design, painting, theatre or architecture in fact bears little relation to the reality. Its writers are inevitably propagandists and move from a modernist standpoint which abhors the academic tradition, realism, romance and revivalism.

A younger generation, I find, has none of these prejudices and is rediscovering a rich native tradition which not even the combined resources of the critics, the Arts Council, the Design Council and the ICA has succeeded in killing off.

Memorial Services

THE LATE Lady Hartwell once said to me: 'Remember, Roy, life after the age of 35 is one long memorial service.' More than a decade on I went to her memorial service, one remarkable for its flowers and for the absence of any eulogistic address. It was vividly reflective of her dislike of humbug and her innate modesty, not easily perceived on first encounter.

Another service, also at St Margaret's, Westminster, which went minus address was for Lord Hood. It brings to mind a conversation I overheard soon afterwards between what must have been two full-time memorial-service-goers: 'Oh, you should have gone instead to Rhoda Birley's. It had specially composed music and John Betjeman chose the hymns.' Did the person who muttered those words, I've often wondered, scour the Court page of *The Times*, deciding which service would be the aesthetic hit of the day?

I must confess to a certain drollery towards it all. There can be no doubt, however, that there has been a vast multiplication in the practice of holding memorial or thanksgiving services in the last few years. The funerals of public figures, unlike a century ago, have become private events and the necessary public expression of grief, memory and celebration has been transferred to the memorial service.

In London four churches virtually monopolize the industry: St Margaret's (mainly political), St Paul's, Covent Garden (theatre and the arts), St Martin-in-the-Fields, and St James's, Piccadilly (taking in what they can). Having lately gone to so many, I am aware that most people have a set of 'black' tucked away in their wardrobes; it is one of the few occasions when women are relatively oblivious to fashion, and old clothes are the norm.

The memorial service is an event neatly timed within an ordered day not to interfere with the morning's work, nor upset any appointment for luncheon at one. It is a muted midday gathering of the establishment and *le monde* to commemorate a gap in its ranks. Sometimes they are wonderful, sometimes they fall flat and sometimes something goes wrong.

Who would ever have thought that the late Marie Rambert's service would have been plagued from start to finish by the noise of a barrel organ outside in the piazza? Or that, as we sat down, the pew would collapse. How she would have loved it! Sometimes an address can go awry. At a service for Benedict Nicolson, Lord Clark, normally an impeccable eulogizer, suddenly launched into an attack on the Bloomsbury Group.

Theatrical services tend to be memorable for everyone involved, including the congregation. Sir Lewis Casson's took place in Westminster Abbey, and I shall always remember the distant echoing voices of the choir singing of paradise, and the sight of Sybil Thorndike in the procession, all in white, smiling and happy like a bride on her wedding day.

Oliver Messel's service brought glimpses of the heroines of one's youth, Evelyn Laye and Dorothy Dickson. But it was notable for the finest memorial address I have ever heard, delivered extempore, it seemed, by Dame Ninette de Valois. A worthier epitaph he could never have wished for than her recollection of an ancient Russian who remarked on seeing his *Sleeping Beauty* in Leningrad, 'Tchaikovsky and Petipa should have been alive to have seen this!'

Cecil Beaton's service, at which I was an usher, was rather flat by comparison. How irritated he would have been to see the pews filling up with so many people I recall him categorizing as 'ghastly'. One of the drawbacks of the memorial service is that it is open house, which means perhaps that there is still something to be said for the funeral. If Beaton's memorial service misfired, his funeral was a triumph. It was extraordinary to walk up to the church with flowers laid on either side of the path, including tributes from so many of his goddesses – Irene Worth, Garbo and, most typical of all, a floral crown from the inimitable Lady Diana Cooper. In this instance I'm glad I went to both.

Fortunately the Church of England still offers its hospitality, its liturgy and its hymns in memory of the agnostic or inactive believer. I never feel happy at those secular gatherings. Bare addresses, perhaps a reading or two, a piece of music and then straight onto the glass of plonk and the chatter. But then it never is comforting to have the vision of eternity removed.

The Demise of Domestics

HAVING SERVANTS these days is an increasingly rare experience. Gone are the days of shock like those of a friend's grandmother who discovered in old age that the milk arrived in bottles, or another elderly woman who never got up because she had no lady's maid. On her bedside table, laid ready to hand, were her two props of life, the Bible and *Debrett*. Or one calls to mind another friend whose mother-in-law held up her hands in horror on learning that there would no longer be a head housemaid, as though that were the wreck of the family's fortunes.

For us humbler souls all this sounds like Ruritania, as the most that the declining upper classes can now aspire to is a hired freelance domestic, or an au pair from the Philippines or Portugal. Anyone who has struggled to leave a telephone message with the latter will warm to the anonymous joys of the answering machine.

The only house where I can actually remember seeing a servants' hall still laid out was Mentmore before its dissolution; the ratio of servants to those seated around the lunch table was almost on a par. Chequers is still copiously staffed but, oddly, by ladies of the armed services, who must be chosen on the criterion that they should not exceed the shoulder height of any visitor. Only the English could give their prime ministers a country house and not even provide a butler.

Being unpacked is therefore a fast-vanishing experience. It is one I always fight off because one can never find anything. My wife always carries her drawing pencils in old Roger & Gallet soap boxes, with the result that in the British Embassy in Paris she found them laid out in patterns all over the bathroom. The late Lady Hartwell sensibly had the inside of her suitcases inscribed with 'Do not unpack this case' in five different languages.

Having clothes laid out also brings its hazards. Lord Ramsey, the former Archbishop of Canterbury, is said to have found his surplice put out for him as a nightshirt. In the late 1960s, when the more *avant* dandies wore kaftans in the evening, I recall some curious incidents as domestics struggled through what would seem a wardrobe of 'dresses' looking for a dinner jacket. One dandy returned to his room to change to find a pair of socks and a blazer on the bed.

Table service is one matter, because we are used to it in restaurants, but incursions into the bedroom to draw curtains, put on lights and light fires, to open windows and run bath water, is another. We are no longer accustomed to it, and when this extends to seizing half one's wardrobe for the laundry, pressing or repairs, the result is bewilderment and a sense of being under siege. How extraordinary it must have been when this was a norm of existence for the establishment classes, as it was until as late as 1939.

Part of London now thrives on a small band of domestics for hire. Often a front door is swung back to reveal the same deferential face that one saw elsewhere the night before. My wife and I used to keep a look-out for one we designated 'the drunken butler' ever since, many years ago, we glimpsed him at Lord Weidenfeld's falling backwards on to a sofa with the entrée in his hands.

I have not seen any recent statistics on domestics, but I would guess that, contrary to what one would think, the number has fallen during the recession. Those households that have them are a rarefied few, and the gap between the lifestyle of the Royal Family and the greater houses must have widened dramatically. All this is reflective not only of declining incomes, but of a change in social attitude on both sides of the green baize door. The only time that a slight yearning crosses my mind is when the flow of conversation at a dinner party is interrupted because the host is also cook and butler.

For nearly everyone the idea of servants has become an embarrassing one. The thought context of previous centuries, when the word 'family' included them, has gone. On the other hand their presence must have allowed the creative minds of an earlier age to work at full stretch. As I iron my shirts and press my trousers, I often think 'Carlyle did not have to do this.'

Birthdays

I REDISCOVERED my birthday at the age of 40. It had interested me up until the age of 25, after which it was virtually banished from my mind for a decade and a half. I fancy that this rediscovery in middle age is not unusual and, now that Christmas has been ruined, it is much more fun and far more unexpected to send friends birthday cards.

'But how did you know?' they all exclaim, for finding out the dates, often dropped by accident in conversation through the year, is quite an art. Then they have to be written into a birthday calendar which has to be pinned up where it can catch the eye in time. Bulk buying of cards becomes an essential part of this pleasurable activity.

The Queen is lucky in having two birthdays and in Catholic countries there is the name-day, which in my mind only evokes Monsieur Triquet reciting his stately poem to Tatiana in *Eugene Onegin*. But, alas, most of us must be content with just one.

Even if I read nothing else in *The Times* I always run my eyes down the birthday column. One reason is the bizarre alignment of people: Lawrence Durrell, 72, Antoinette Sibley, 45, and Elizabeth Taylor, 52, all on February 27. One's own birthday is shared by the unlikely assortment of Gene Kelly, Carl Dolmetsch and Lord Kissin. The other, far from charitable, reason is to tot up just how long this or that person has to run in office. And then there is the ultimate mystery of who choses who gets in.

Old age, on the whole, is the cruellest joke of all, so it is always bewildering that the older public figures become, the higher their ratings on the birthday applausometer. After the age of 70 the British forgive virtually everyone for everything, and the long-livers enter their apogee. Lady Diana Cooper, the Earl of Stockton, and, above all, the Queen Mother enter the league-table of birthdays evoking semi-national festivals in which they are approximated to their ideal selves amid a blaze of publicity. It is, however, a curious line of argument that equates the completion of nine decades of existence with an earldom.

In respect of long-livers, my most memorable overheard conversation on this subject of birthdays was between Lord Drogheda and the late Dame Marie Rambert. The latter, athletic to the end, rushed up the aisle of the Royal Opera House and butted in, saying: 'I'll be 91 in four weeks time'. 'So what', came the withering reply. 'Sir Robert Mayer will be 100 in June and you'll never catch him up.'

That centennial was marked by a splendid concert in the Festival Hall, which brings me to the subject of parties. The redoubtable Christobel, Lady Aberconway, made a great cult of her birthday, so much so that her famous party stretched over two days by the close of her life. I caught them in their final phase when she sat with her onyx-handled walking stick beside her beneath a tree in her Mayfair garden receiving the annual obeisance of *le monde*. So crowded had it become that guests spent most of the time stepping back into the pond.

Lord Weidenfeld ushered in his fiftieth year in the 1970s with a party in 'exotic dress'. Unfortunately, the pious wife of one recipient of an invitation misread this as 'erotic dress' and tore it up. I remember going as Aubrey Beardsley's vision of the Regency, carrying a vast fur muff, and the event was a monument to vanished opulence. To the same era belonged a long series of annual birthday parties given by Mrs Henry J.

Heinz in honour of her husband. These included a party on a boat which sailed up to Greenwich, remarkable because two ladies appeared wearing exactly the same expensive dress and were unable to avoid each other, and another at Regent's Park Zoo to which we were bidden to come disguised as animals, which evoked some very curious results.

When a relative died a few years ago we found the whole year's birthday cards all neatly signed, sealed and stamped with a note attached to each telling the domestic when to post it. For that person the magic had evaporated. For me it still remains and every year I love opening every silly card lifting a hand to the passing of time, and being thankful for the endurance through it of so much friendship and affection.

St George's Day

I WRITE this on April 23, St George's Day, and his ensign – a red cross on a white ground – flutters from many a local parish flagpole, reflecting Anglican loyalty to a saint demoted by the Church of Rome. In the past, this was the day of the Garter procession, when the sovereign, regardless of where he resided, passed in gorgeous cavalcade attended by his knights through the palace courtyard to the Chapel Royal. In Tudor times this was a great public event and so it remained until Charles I, who was what *1066 and All That* should have categorized as a 'Bad Thing', moved it to Windsor. Now the event remains sadly and permanently divorced from the day and its historic context, living on as a spectacle to launch Ascot week, in June.

I have seen the Garter procession only twice. Once from the roof of the Round Tower as I rushed from one side to the other as the stately procession meandered its way down to St George's Chapel. A second time more grandly from the eaves of what was Lord Charteris's house thronged with *le monde* and with strawberries for tea. Knights of the Garter tend to be advanced in years and my main memory consists of a blast of wind which seemed to blow most of them over to an almost impossible angle so that I thought they would all topple like the pack of cards in *Alice in Wonderland*. As the procession returned uphill there were those who were gathered into limousines in case they fell by the wayside.

Like Lord Bute in the eighteenth century, it is an advantage to have good legs to be a Garter Knight. In full evening dress they wear their Garter with kneebreeches and black silk stockings. I once glimpsed the new Lord Wilson cutting a fetching figure thus attired.

But how extraordinary it is that after 600 years this ceremony still exerts its potent spell as a manifestation of royalist chivalry flooding down the centuries and that we can still see pass before us a cavalcade that inspired the brush of Van Dyck and the pencil of Lely. Their visions inevitably romanticized the original, but how fascinating it is that in revamped terms the crown's use of chivalry remains unchanged in its objective of uniting divergent viewpoints into a single *hommage à la reine*. For under these velvet robes and beplumed hats stride the unlikely figures, not only of Lord Wilson, but Lord Drogheda, Lord Longford and the Duke of Grafton, to name but four. As those who have held office as prime minister twice are usually accorded the honour, we can expect to see Mrs Thatcher join this loyal band, for which ladies wear the Garter on their arm.

Besides Garter glories, April 23 calls to mind Shakespeare's birthday. There is still something wonderful about a second procession, that to Holy Trinity, Stratford-upon-Avon. In 1964 it was the four hundredth anniversary of his birth and I walked in that procession clutching a bouquet of sweet herbs – rosemary and thyme and sage – a poet's nosegay. By the time I reached the church the chancel was piled high with flowers, cascades of bloom dappled with sunlight and the organ blazing forth in glory.

That was the year of the great Shakespeare Exhibition at Stratford, which began with such high hopes and ended in disaster. The portraits and documents fell under my aegis and even they were doomed to the last. As I sat down next to some African dignitary at the launching luncheon a note was passed to me. Unfolding it I read: 'We've lost Shakespeare's will.'

That nearly ruined that particular April 23.

It was the old Duke of Newcastle who told Charles II at the Restoration that 'ceremony though it is nothing in itself yet it doth everything'. In many ways this is very true and the British have a genius for it, largely because there has been no disruption to the tradition since the seventeenth century. But it is only so when ritual is a true expression of ideals and beliefs shared by both actors and onlookers. When the two part company it is reduced to an empty charade. It is such a parting of the ways that those who take part in such spectacles must forever guard against. 'For what is a King', Newcastle went on to say, 'more than a subject but for ceremony and order. When that fails him he's ruined.'

Homage to the Heralds

A FRIEND presented us with a wedding gift: a seventeenth-century paper-cut picture of William Camden, antiquarian and Clarenceux King of Arms. 'The last good herald', we were told. Looking around the hall of the College of Arms at the dinner in 1984 to commemorate their 500th anniversary, I felt this pronouncement a little unjust. From the walls peered down at us from canvas and panel the faces of generations of heralds from Tudor times to the present, while around the table our hosts were identifiable by the enamelled medallion of the royal arms they wore.

One of the heralds extraordinary opposite me explained that there was at present no room for any more of them as they had run out of tabards. I had always wondered about these marvellous garments ever since first encountering them in Tenniel's illustrations to Lewis Carroll. Apparently they cost no less than £20,000 each to make, and heralds on state occasions are laced into them. This in itself is interesting because it preserves a medieval way of fastening clothes, universal before the advent of the button, let alone the zip fastener. Stiff with gold embroidery, they must virtually stand up on their own and their weight must be considerable.

The very names of the heralds and pursuivants have always mesmerized me: Garter, Clarenceux, Portcullis, Richmond, Bluemantle, Rouge Croix, Norroy and Ulster. Add to them those who act as extraordinaries bearing titles appertaining to the Earl Marshal: Norfolk, Arundel and Maltravers.

It is almost thirty years since I had my first contact with what was then a mysterious institution, the College of Arms in London's Queen Victoria Street. I had come across a reference to score-sheets for Elizabethan tournaments in their possession, for in the sixteenth century heralds acted in the same way as those who keep score at cricket today. That occasion was my initial encounter with Sir Anthony Wagner, whose magisterial *Heralds of England* appeared in 1967. But my main memory is his lament over the problems posed by including miner's lamps in coats-of-arms.

What one notices most looking back since then, however, is the enormous change in attitude on the part of that ancient institution and its inmates. It has voyaged from being what struck one as an inward looking clique guarding inherited prerogatives to one which is acutely aware of its role as keeper of a mighty tradition that embraces not only the minutiae of genealogy and of arms, besides the meticulous details of ceremonial, but is also aware of a wider national commitment. That was embodied in the appeal to create a separate museum of heraldry in which the College's treasures could be shown to the public. Although that never materialized in its original bold form, it came to fruition in more modest manner in the present display in the Tower of London.

Knowledge of the rudiments of heraldry as part of the make-up of the average educated person is in retreat and that perhaps ought to be remedied. Where, for instance, would English art be without it? It is saturated with heraldry wherever one looks in any building, secular or ecclesiastical. Heraldry too is the only part of the repertory of decoration to survive the onslaught of the modernist movement, for no designer can tamper with a coat-of-arms. To do so is to erode an identity.

It was Lincoln Kirstein who once remarked, having seen, if I remember rightly, Churchill's funeral, that the Earl Marshal was the world's greatest choreographer. The observation was an acute one, even if it might come as a surprise to the present Duke of Norfolk to be bracketed with Petipa and Balanchine. To my eye our genius in the dance stems as much as anything from our inherent feeling for ordered ceremonial.

In the field of state occasions the heralds are keepers of the choreographic notation for these events. Their archives record each procession, in terms of its order, its dress and symbolic attribute. Every movement of the body is noted: the bearing of attributes from crowns to wands of office, bowing in deference or kneeling in fealty. All of these ingredients brought together and orchestrated give us the tremendous crowd scenes which make up a state funeral, wedding or a coronation, drawing them into a web of history.

Brains and the British

THE BRITISH do not like intellectuals. Rather, let us be accurate, they do not like intellectuals who fail to conceal that they are. The exception, of course, is those who have a foreign name. I have always thought that my life would have been completely different if my surname had been Strongski. With that *nom de plume* and an accent, preferably gutteral Germanic, audiences would sit mesmerized by my every utterance. The late Dr Jacob Bronowski's career was entirely built around this British cult of the foreign professor. Millions sat glued to their television sets listening to material which, if delivered by one of their countrymen, they would have instantly switched off.

This is not meant in any way to deny brilliance or contribution. Indeed we would be greatly the poorer without them. It is merely a comment upon a curious attitude which we have that evokes untold reverence for exiled intellectuals or those whose advent barely goes back more than a generation. It is a pantheon which gathers to itself such stars in the cerebral firmament as George Steiner, Sir Isaiah Berlin, Sir Ernst Gombrich, Lord Kaldor or Lord Weidenfeld. But it is also an attitude which belongs to a wider context.

When I was at school in the 1950s it was certainly ground into me that British painting was on the whole foreign: Holbein, Van Dyck and Kneller covered the period down to about 1700 after which, apart from Hogarth, Constable and Turner, there wasn't much to compete with the statement that all painting was French. The same was true of sculpture, running from Rysbrack and Roubiliac down to, yes, Jacob Epstein. Equally it was applied to music, defined wholly in terms of Handel and Mendelssohn and the visits of Mozart and Haydn to England. And all opera was Italian.

So too was this true of the ballet. That was Russian or, at a pinch, French. The result of this insular fixation was that the pioneers of our ballet had to change their names to be taken seriously at all: Ninette de Valois, Marie Rambert, Anton Dolin, Markova and Fonteyn. It must have been a brave decision at that period to have hung onto names as ordinary as Harold Turner and Mona Inglesby.

All fashion was French. So were all hairdressers, with salons labelled Maison or Madame X. Food and restaurants were almost uniformly French and nothing has shifted French from the menu cards of the grandest tables.

It is some measure of the past 30 years that virtually all this has been reversed. The Americans discovered British art, which now occupies a position as seminal within a world context as that of any other European nation. The Royal Ballet has made dance British and the fashion explosion of the 1960s has shattered the one-way road to Paris. The rediscovery of early English music and the achievements of Benjamin Britten alone have restored our musical mythology. Even British cooks and menus in English are now making headway.

'A rose by any other name ...'? It is not quite as simple as that. We stand at the end of centuries of fixed preconceptions. Up until the past few decades we have never thought in terms of intellectual or cultural 'empire' as the Italians, and above all the French, always have. Horace Walpole summed up our viewpoint neatly in the eighteenth century when he wrote in respect of the arts: 'This country does not always err in vaunting its own productions.' In fact the rediscovery of our past achievements and our reclamation in the present runs exactly parallel with our loss of the empire of power. The only one left to us is the one of intellect and art sustained, above all, by English becoming a universal *lingua franca*. So that our reconquest of areas we used cheerfully, even disdainfully, to assign to foreigners has a deeper significance than we would at first admit.

It is also a result of the reverse of what it was hoped would emerge from joining the EEC. The sinking of national identity into Europe, besides leading to an intensification of the cult of the crown, has led us to focus with fervency on what we can identify as uniquely ours. For the first time in our history we stand at the centre of a cultural empire. But it is basically one of the arts, for these we have learnt to respect. It has yet to happen in the world of learning and of the intellect.

Word for word
the quick brow
the lazy black dog
lazy black dog
Tuesday

Writing and Typing

Diaries

Penguin Books

Children's Stories

Tablescapes

The Lecturer's Art

Writing and Typing

AMERICAN academic friends now write letters to me on word processors. At first I took no notice, but now I progressively realize that the time is fast approaching when I shall have to bid farewell to that beloved Olivetti Lettera 22 that I have bashed so mercilessly since I purchased it, as an impoverished student, in 1956. Space will have to be found to come to terms with an aspect of the new technology in one's own daily life. Failing which one will appear an old dodo by the end of the century.

This is all the stranger in that the advent and acceptability of the typewriter as a means of personal correspondence is still so relatively recent. There hovers around it yet many fine gradations governing correct social etiquette that subtly dictate whether fingers should be put to the keys or to the pen. Bread and butter thank-you notes are handwritten, as if that were a measure of their sincerity, which it is not. Anyone who uses a typewriter knows those moments of hesitation and decision.

As the typewriter becomes an antique we can already categorize not only the machines and the type faces, but what it produces. At the moment the fashion is not to indent for paragraphs, and the full stop, apart from at the end of a sentence, has been totally eliminated as a form of punctuation.

Typewriters anyway have their own hierarchy, the basic premise of which is the grander the person in social rank, the larger the type face. Letters emanating from the Royal Household or 10 Downing Street truly epitomize luxurious eighteenth-century indulgence, with gargantuan letters floating through the proverbial meadow of margin. The effect is to make even the most commonplace communication of magisterial import. This is true style, as much as any form of linking italic type or the use of a sepia ribbon is not. Those unfortunate lapses in taste join the use of green or violet pen ink.

Every generation, when taught to write, must have been subjected to some sort of calligraphic reforming movement. In the immediate postwar period I remember being taught italic script, although why in the late 1940s it seemed forward-looking to model one's handwriting on a fifteenth-century Italian cursive script, with a preference for papal Chancery italic, I have never been able to fathom. It has left its mark, and I can still manage a debased version when writing an inscription or dedication.

The way handwriting slips into generational categories never ceases to fascinate. The age of a correspondent can almost invariably be guessed from the formation of the letters. Those over 70 who caught the tail-end of Victorian copperplate discipline give way to the illegible inter-war product.

When we can become so easily our own mini-Caxtons, other people's handwriting can be a curse. The National Art-Collections Fund provided instances of people still running an organization with handwritten letters. To unravel a letter from the late Lord Crawford, who headed the fund, was always a major operation. Once the whole V & A office spent a week trying to decipher something handwritten. In the end the letter was sent back to his secretary, in hope of elucidation. No, she couldn't read it either, and his lordship was on holiday.

Of recent communicants, Jean Muir sticks in the mind as having a script which produces five staccato words to the page and which is best unravelled by pinning it up and looking at it from a distance. It is worth deciphering, but too many unreadable letters are not. Even more maddening are illegible signatures to typed letters or just a christian name, like John, defying identification out of the 20 in the address book. That agony reaches a crescendo with postcards and Christmas cards which carry no address at all.

Anyone who has struggled with the handwriting of the past will therefore join with me in raising a hand in salute to the typewriter as it is about to pass into the museum showcase. I think of the hours attempting to read a menu for Richard II's coronation banquet in medieval Latin, with its strange contractions, as part of a palaeography class concerned with court and secretary hands. How envious one was of those who researched into any period after the Civil War, when handwriting suddenly seemed to enter a long period of over two centuries of legibility, while medievalists and Tudor historians toiled away at pages seemingly written by a short-sighted fly. Out of all those scripts I still recall that of Francis Bacon's secretary writing French as my palaeographic Waterloo.

Diaries

DIARY WRITING is a strange art. We seem to be seized with diary mania: Nicolson, Beaton, Channon, Waugh, Crossman and now Peter Hall. The public seems to have an insatiable appetite for the genre. Newspapers cannot wait to serialize the revelations, and those who appear in them must finger them nervously, wondering whether to telephone the lawyer. I well remember the glee of one celebrated diarist as he contemplated the annoyance his next volume would provoke. It is difficult to believe, however, that this is the spirit in which the greatest diaries of the past were written.

Not every reader can have lifted his head from the Hall diaries with a happy glow. Many would emerge in a mood far different. What becomes more interesting, as has been noted, is the narrowing gap between writing and publication, in this case only just over three years from the last entry in 1980.

It is not, however, the gap that matters so much as what is written. After all there was only a four-year divide before the last of Cecil Beaton's diaries appeared, but their content, though often perceptive, was anodyne. And the famous 'Jennifer' publishes her diary monthly in *Harpers and Queen*, evoking no cries of anguish at all. Again it is related to content, although one day someone will break the code for this particular diary and discover what those recurring adjectives such as 'delightful' actually mean.

The howl produced by Hall's diaries was related to another fact: they were not political. Over the last 20 years we have grown to accept the publication of political diaries and memoirs by everyone from Richard Crossman and Barbara Castle to Marcia Falkender. And very boring they usually are, too. Peter Hall's diaries, however, lift the curtain as never before on the world of the subsidized arts. Far from visions of aesthetic loveliness and delight and all our backstage romances being fulfilled, we are presented instead with sordid battles and intrigues.

The saddest thing of all is that theatre as magic is destroyed for us by a man who has so conspicuously contributed so much of that very ingredient over the years.

As diaries, however, they belong firmly to the stream-of-consciousness class as against the considered observation of people and events. Fortunately the diaries which our descendants will cherish are yet to come. For when it comes to reading a diary for pure pleasure or as literature, it is surely those which watch social detail that most entrance. That is why, for instance, Pepys will always score over Evelyn.

As time becomes more distant the revelations and rows which so excite us become meaningless, but the account of clothes, places, events, food and customs becomes hypnotic. Any contemporary diary that recorded precisely this aspect would probably be unpublishable because, to a degree, it is recording what we can still see around us. Only when that is no longer so would it be of interest.

A diary of a present-day Parson Woodforde or Rev. Francis Kilvert would therefore have to wait for a period. One is, I hope, being written somewhere, for such diaries are the true and rarest jewels of the art, a chronicle of the ordinary. Woodforde's panorama of the village life of late eighteenth-century Norfolk rings with truthfulness. I love those endless menus: 'gave them for dinner, a Couple of Chicken boiled and a

Tongue, a Leg of Mutton boiled and Capers and Batter Pudding for the first Course. Second, a couple of Ducks roasted and green Peas, some Artichokes, Tarts and Blancmange.' The same applies to the immortal evocation of rural Herefordshire by Kilvert, with its perfect mirror of daily life and character and the cycle of the seasons.

It is the diaries alone which have lifted these people from the dust and made them immortal. Their motivation was not false pride or paying off old scores, which seem to be the principal driving force behind virtually all contemporary contributions to the art. Hall's diaries made me take down my own from the shelf and ponder deeply on the vices of such a literary form.

Penguin Books

THE BOOKS that first stir the eye and the intellect are ones that remain through life peculiarly precious. *British Military Uniforms* by James Laver was given to me by a friend on my thirteenth birthday, in 1948. It introduced me to the serious history of dress, of which the author was a pioneer, and it was my first King Penguin. In 1985 we celebrate the half-centenary of that publishing house, and what an enormous bouquet those of my generation owe to Allen Lane.

Everyone will have his own memories, his own debts to express. Mine centres very much on the King Penguin series, now collectors' items (we've nearly completed our set) but then, in the dark days of the war and its austerity aftermath, among the few modestly priced art books with colour plates. What a debt one owes to Carl Winter's *Elizabethan Miniatures*, which cost just three shillings. Published in 1943, its reproductions of portraits by Holbein, Hilliard and Oliver were pored over during my teens and became the source from which was to flow an obsession with the art of Shakespeare's England that has lasted forty years.

Before one had even seen a ballet on stage, Janet Leeper's *English Ballet*, with plates of designs by Rex Whistler, Nadia Benois and Leslie Hurry, had fed the imagination. And then there were ones like Pevsner's *The Leaves of Southwell* and M. D. Anderson's *Misericords* that awoke one's interest in English churches. As in the case of that other wartime series, *Britain in Pictures*, they were essentially insular in outlook and must have been seminal for a younger generation in kindling an interest in our own historic environment. Ironically the editor of the series was an exile, Nikolaus Pevsner, whose later work, especially *The Englishness of English Art* and the great *Buildings of England* series, seems such a natural outcome.

Penguins were also responsible for one's earliest awareness of contemporary art. The King Penguin on the Romney Marsh, illustrated and described by John Piper, resulted in a sustained period of Piper pastiche with crayon and watercolour in one's art class. More important was another series, Penguin Modern Painters, this time at three shillings and sixpence. Piper again, of course, but also Stanley Spencer, Duncan Grant, Ben Nicholson, Henry Moore, Matthew Smith, Paul Nash, Graham Sutherland and many more.

And what authors! John Betjeman, Raymond Mortimer, Herbert Read, Clive Bell and Edward Sackville-West. There were few exhibitions then. The great art galleries were only just struggling to reopen so that these tiny books with their plates were one's Tate Gallery.

And when I went up to university to read history in 1953, once again a series inspired me, this time *The Pelican History of England*. Shyly one sat at the feet of S. T. Bindoff, author of the volume on *Tudor England*, which had appeared only three years before. It is still in print. The book had flashes of magic that lit my imagination. Two lines stick in the mind. One in the epilogue when he describes the end of Gloriana: 'But life, that long-lasting fire before which she had warmed her splendid hands, was sinking and she made ready to depart.' (It was only years later that I discovered that he had lifted it from Walter Savage Landor.) The other was the opening phrase of the biography of the author which appeared on the back of the book: 'S. T. Bindoff has enjoyed a career remarkable chiefly for its uneventfulness.'

Not long after came a period of flat-sharing and the advent of cooking. Elizabeth David's *A Book of Mediterranean Food* and *French Country Cooking*, my two earliest purchases, are still in use, stained and spattered as the pages are by my experiments. The former I marked up at the time with a cross by every recipe I thought possible, although I never did essay *Filet de Porc en Sanglier*. Classics as these are, how well they encapsulate an era when the middle classes had to learn to cook, and travel to the continent was possible again. The author's opening line to her 1955 preface says it all: 'This book first appeared in 1950, when almost every essential ingredient of good cooking was either rationed or unobtainable.' Both, incidentally, were illustrated by John Minton, introducing one to contemporary book illustration and reminding one also of the enormous contribution Penguin made in that field.

This is a personal anthology. It could be far longer both in terms of content and time span. But it is a tribute to those who fed a young inquisitive mind and eye during a period of deprivation. They were the publishers who gave to those who, like myself, were able to go to the university as a result of the post-war Education Acts, the opportunity of forming a modest library. Need one say more?

Children's Stories

WHENEVER I feel particularly gloomy I retreat to a tiny bedroom on the far side of the house with rose-besprinkled wallpaper and walls hung with the sentimental prints found in a 1930s nursery. Intuitively one turns to reverie in that arcadian haven on the next step back to the womb, the books of childhood. No others exert quite the healing spell of these simplistic narratives in which virtue triumphs in the end, in which the word-content is often minimal, and in which pictures cast a potent magic over the imagination. Here is a timeless and utterly secure world.

Fishing books off the shelves at random is generally a short-lived expedition. Belonging to a generation brought up in the 1940s, it is inevitable that one pulls out *The Railway Children*, *Ballet Shoes*, *The Secret Garden*, one of the endless books about the Famous Five or *Swallows and Amazons*. The way of life they present, looked at in retrospect, seems appallingly smug and bourgeois. At the time, however, that seemed not to matter as one read or heard them dramatized on the wireless in a room whose windows were criss-crossed with brown sticky paper to avoid splintering glass from bomb blast, and hung with funereal black curtains. Instead they fed a young mind with a repertory of images and aspirations, of houses, gardens, travel and theatre, all things unexperienced as a result of the incarceration of wartime childhood.

Almost half-a-century on, how ambivalent is one's attitude to their mythology. With a plague of rabbits in the garden, *The Tale of the Flopsy Bunnies* makes one wonder whether it is not responsible for all the rabbit rescues I carry out from the jaws of our cat. And when I catch a mole I try hard not to think of *The Wind in the Willows* or Alison Uttley's Moldy Warp, a character in her Little Grey Rabbit books.

The marvellous thing about children's books is that once a formula has been established, they go on for long periods of time and then enter the orbit of classics that are forever reprinted. They remain irresistible books to purchase still. Oddly, it is not Grimm or the fairy tales that interest me any more, but the indigenous publications. That is explicable, because they are set in a world we know or which we can just recall.

Delightful though they remain, one can see just why the stories of Ameliaranne Stiggins seem so dated. The visitor to the great house, filling her green umbrella with cakes for her impoverished family, belongs firmly to a pre-1914 feudalism that Kate Greenaway, Beatrix Potter or A. A. Milne somehow managed to sidestep.

It is oddly comforting moving in a world of bears with 'very little brain' or cats like the marvellous marmalade Orlando. Their adventures invariably put things to rights, their eye-level is low like a child's and both natural phenomena and man-made artefacts are huge. One can understand why the late Poet Laureate hung onto his teddy bear.

In middle-age, when the world so often seems blighted, to let the eye meander through these pages is oddly consoling. Perhaps, behind that mousehole in the wainscot, there really is a mini-house full of mice in tiny dresses and trousers living a life not so different from our own. Perhaps the cat does have an existence I don't know about, in which, like Orlando, he ends up wearing a vast curled wig, sitting in court on a blotter with a watch strapped to his tail. And shouldn't I, like Pooh, always be counting those jars of honey in the kitchen cupboard just in case it has been raided by honey-mad bears overnight? Better, while I am about it, check the marmalade too in case Paddington has got in.

Perhaps the key to these books is precisely that quality, their ability still to trigger such fantasy in even the adult mind. As I grew up I foolishly discarded all my childhood books, an act which now I deeply regret. Fortunately my wife kept hers. How glad I am that she did.

Tablescapes

In a recent series of lectures on interior decoration I was particularly struck by a view of a room in an apartment of an American decorator, Keith Irvine. Tables in proximity to easy chairs had been replaced by piles of large books. Recalling the 1960s cult of the coffee table book it seemed, on reflection, a logical development to dispense with the table altogether and replace it by the books.

The deployment of books in relation to people I find one of the most revealing of studies. From the arrangement and use of them within an interior one can usually build up a pretty accurate picture of the person. Or can one? For in the main what one sees is a slight variation upon a single theme of what has become a stylistic commonplace of upper class life.

I have often wondered who was the person to introduce books on a lavish scale into the drawing room. Who was it during the 1960s who first placed that circular table with its fringed cloth to the ground on which piles of books were arranged to instil in the visitor a knowledge of the owner's taste and discernment in literature and the arts? By the close of that decade it had become a cliché of room arrangement. I can remember one such 'tablescape' – by David Hicks – in which art books were placed in a pattern so that if one actually moved as much as a single volume the design of the room was ruined.

It is what goes on to those tables which is so fascinating. There must always be the catalogue of what is regarded as *the* art exhibition of moment. Dutch painting gives way to Renoir, Stubbs to Chagall. Biographies of contemporaries or near contemporaries provide a certain aura indicating connection or acquaintanceship. For a decade the staple was a succession of volumes with yet more dreary revelations about the Bloomsbury circle. Now it is biographies of recent establishment figures such as Kenneth Clark.

All forms of royal biography of the top league variety by a Frances Donaldson or Kenneth Rose are a *sine qua non*. Books on country houses and gardens, both at home and abroad, establish that the owner has at least visited if not stayed in most of them. John Martin Robinson's *The Latest Country Houses* has supplanted Clive Aslet's *The Last Country Houses*. Older glossies such as Nigel Nicolson's *Great Houses of Britain* and Mark Girouard's *Life in the English Country House* are virtually part of the fittings.

For those with literary pretensions, Anita Brookner's *Hotel du Lac* was for months a certain ingredient. All forms of paperback, except very expensive ones, are out. Whether any of this great array is read it would be interesting to know but it is certainly looked at.

Books in bedrooms are another story and many a hostess must spend most of Friday trundling the heaps from room to room. The mainstays of these are invariably diaries, books of short stories, and novels. James Lees-Milne's *Ancestral Voices*, with its witty descriptions of disintegrating country houses and even more disintegrating owners, epitomizes the genre. Cecil Beaton's diaries fall into the same bracket, as do those by Chips Channon, Harold Nicolson and Noel Coward. Their contents provide in snippets what the contents of the table downstairs give in sustained prose.

Loo books add a further dimension. Those fortunate enough to be sent John Julius Norwich's *A Christmas Cracker* possess the ultimate chic in this field. Books of cartoons by

Osbert Lancaster and Marc, anything illustrated by Sir Hugh Casson and a recent spate of books by Debrett as to what constitutes the make-up of the English upper classes are standard ingredients. Indeed the little room might be said to be consecrated to the literature dedicated to the elucidation of the Sloane Ranger.

Like the invitations on the mantleshelf or the magazines and papers laid out on the stool before the country house fire, the common denominator of these books provides a fascinating index as to the make-up and preoccupations of the establishment classes. As soon as such books migrate from the drawing room and bedroom tables and graduate to the bookshelf, taste and fashion have moved on.

The Lecturer's Art

THE EARLIEST public lecture I ever gave was at the Victoria and Albert Museum in 1958. Crippled with shyness in the face of that huge lecture theatre, I held forth on 'Pageantry in the Elizabethan Court Year'. As the microphone was hung around my neck I began to get nervous of getting entangled in its wires. 'Don't worry about that', the Keeper of Public Relations said, 'just swish it behind you like a dowager swishes her train.' As soon as the lights dimmed and the slides began everything went swimmingly as one was oblivious of the audience. Afterwards an ancient couple tottered up to me and said, 'Oh, thank you, thank you, it was so marvellous.' I have never looked back since.

Over two and half decades on I can claim to have endured every form of triumph and tribulation that can be associated with this particular type of communication. I have turned towards the screen only to see the image upon it slowly melt and slide off (no cooler in the projector). I have turned up and found variants of no lectern, no screen, virtually no audience.

The projector has exploded. The electric plug has gone up in flames. I have been expected not only to lecture in pitch darkness but also to push the slides through simultaneously. I once even gave a lecture in a nonconformist pulpit, to be rewarded after by a cheese sandwich preserved beneath a glass dome. So exasperated I became at one time that a list of needs went ahead on a roneoed sheet. Even this did not work. Experience of the United States taught me that early arrival and dress rehearsal is the only thing that will.

Lecturing is the nearest thing an academic experiences to being in repertory as an odd branch of the performing arts. Over the years, like theatre, it depends heavily on repeats and revivals. At the university one noticed the yellowing edges to many a lecture script exhumed from the filing cabinet, much as one glimpses sermon notes from afar. My wife still cherishes one standby in my repertory. Called 'Problem Portraits', it stood me in good stead for a decade until I had mastered every pause and inflexion. I have never indulged in John Betjeman's standard practice of putting in at least one slide upside down.

Any form of questions from the audience after a lecture should be avoided. They invariably turn out to be a vehicle for the ill-informed and opinionated. One Saturday afternoon lecture on Henry VIII at the National Portrait Gallery led to a disquisition on the virtues of vegetarianism (they all ate too much red meat) followed by 'Everything was all right until that woman came along' – gesturing at a portrait of Anne Boleyn.

I flee other people's lectures these days and certainly do not expect anyone to listen to mine. But looking back over the years stars do stick in the mind. A. J. P. Taylor and Sir John Summerson, with never a note in sight, fluent and every detail exact. A. L. Rowse as a kind of Donald Wolfit of the lecture circuit on the battle of Bosworth. Dame Frances Yates, living up to her claimed descent from the actress Mrs Yates, beginning a lecture on the history of the art of memory by describing a mnemonic image which included someone clutching a goat's testicles, at which point she paused, threw her eyes heavenwards and mused, 'A vivid image'. Doris Langley Moore on her life with Byron, holding her audience enthralled from the opening anecdote in which she warded off the advances of a young man at her first dance by abruptly asking him, 'Have you ever read *Childe Harold*?'

In a way, lecturing is to learning what acting is to the play text. It is a marriage of content with interpretative performance, although one never ceases to be amazed how much the latter can triumph in the face of the absence of the former but never in reverse. Not without reason one sometimes emerges from these occasions recalling the words of an American professor to a student who had just delivered a paper on Edmund Spenser: 'Little girl, you have said many new things, and many true things, but your new things are not true and your true things are not new.'

It still astonishes me that people actually want to go to a lecture, for, as a form of communication, it seems so primeval in the technological age in which we live. On the other hand perhaps we ought after all to be grateful that, in spite of all the erosion by the media in the last half century, there is still something hypnotic about someone just standing there and talking.

THE SWISH
OF THE
CURTAIN

Theatre Programmes

Disasters on Stage

Curtain Calls

Sir Frederick Ashton

The Revival of Elgar

Fifty Years of Glyndebourne

Theatre Programmes

THERE WAS a time when one could go to the theatre and cheerfully leave one's brains at the box office, or at least not expect to exert them until the curtain arose on some cerebral drama. That, alas, is no more the case. One of the most remarkable changes in theatre-going over the last two decades has been in programme format. These have escalated from the post-war folded sheet into large quarto booklets which really ought to be issued with the tickets so that the contents can be assimilated before the performance.

I have kept all my theatre programmes since 1948. In terms of space the story is akin to that of sale room catalogues, which also suddenly, at the beginning of the 1960s, began to expand in size until the collection for a single year equalled that for half a decade of the 1940s. The Old Vic programmes of the Guthrie era were modest enough with their yellow outsides and within the cast list, short biographies of artists and the scene sequence. No sign of directorial polemic here.

The change, as far as I can pinpoint it rummaging through the shelves, came during the Peter Hall-Peter Brook regime at the Royal Shakespeare Company. The new approach to staging Shakespeare, under the impact of those who grew up under the post-war education system, suddenly called for gloss. I alighted upon a programme for *Richard II* at Stratford in 1964. It contains a crash course in European kingship. Quotes from Talleyrand, James Baldwin and Albert Camus are accompanied somewhat oddly by the note, 'These short comments ... do not necessarily reflect the ideas of the Royal Shakespeare

Company. They sometimes suggest an oblique or even contrary angle of vision.' We are then given extracts from a conversation with the three directors, short articles on 'The Cycle of a Curse', 'A New Order of Kingship' and 'Who is Richard II?', along with photographs of illuminations from chronicles, the play in rehearsal and previous productions.

What one is looking at is a revolution in the nature of a programme. Twenty years on we are so used to this that one now begins to feel quite irritated if it is not provided. The approach soon spread. Hall took it to the National Theatre where again programmes are stuffed with material. Even the musical *Guys and Dolls* evokes an analysis of Damon Runyon's place in popular literature, his reflection of the realities of American criminal life, and articles on Frank Loesser and the development of the musical besides the inevitable rehearsal photographs.

Sadler's Wells Opera as it transformed itself into ENO at the Coliseum soon followed. Pulling out a programme for their production of Massenet's *Manon* in 1979, I found '*Manon* and its Historical Background', 'The Composition and Style of *Manon*'. Mercifully, opera programmes tend to spare us the rehearsal photographs. Interestingly the Royal Opera House has, on the whole, been shy of taking its programmes the way of an Open University lecture on the subject.

What are we to make of all this? It seems to me to have sprung inevitably from directors who needed to put over new ideas and new concepts to an audience they wanted to capture but which they also recognized to be, by the 1960s, better educated. At their best, programmes have developed as an art-form in their own right in excess of mere printed ephemera. Often their design and lay-out is extremely good, making use of an abundance of visual, historical and literary material that excites the eye and mind for what is to follow. Above all one is delighted to have a theatrical experience cast into a broader perspective.

On the other hand there lingers the danger of what was once innovatory quickly becoming cliché. Is it really so very exciting to have all those obligatory photographs of actors in old clothes rehearsing? Do we always need to be burdened with the never-ending biographies of everyone who has contributed? In some cases this now stretches on for pages and I really cannot believe that the fact that someone was born in Birkenhead is really of much importance. Nor does one want to be over-swamped with lists of sponsors and patrons.

The result is a theatre of two if not three worlds. There are the cerebral companies providing for an intellectual audience. There is the commercial theatre fighting shy of it, conceding only a wrap-around magazine section of total banality. And, finally, there is breadline theatre where one gets handed or picks up – shades of the 1940s – a Roneoed sheet. But in that one moves in the world of the committed. In short, programmes are a remarkably accurate reflection of the journey of British theatre over the last few decades into providing for what are two worlds of comprehension.

Disasters on Stage

SITTING NEAR Lord Drogheda in the royal box at Covent Garden was always an event. One waited for the moment when he produced a little torch and scribbled what became known as a Droghedegram. Never was he more busy, I recall, than during a performance of *Coq d'Or* when a singer's crown came off, at which point she handed it to her attendant. Worse followed, for when the attendant had to move she promptly handed it back, much to the former wearer's surprise. A great carpet was then meant to be unrolled but that too proved to be disaster.

For the lay person in the audience there is always something hypnotic about watching something go wrong. The root of the fascination resides in the ability or otherwise to rescue the situation beneath a blaze of light and before a thousand eyes. Events offstage, such as Carabosse's chariot in *Sleeping Beauty* getting a parking ticket in Floral Street, do not have the same public consequences as its wheel falling off on the first night.

I suppose my earliest memory of such an incident must be a production of *Dick Whittington* in the mid-Forties in which the ship in the harbour scene had been pushed on too far, revealing that only half of it existed. Once, years later, the Christmas tree in *Nutcracker* grew until it vanished almost completely into the fly gallery, only to be lowered back again before an awestruck Clara. So thrown was she that in the ensuing voyage she kept her woollen leg warmers on. And I will long remember the agonies a porter in *Macbeth* went through at the Old Vic as the portcullis stuck.

There is a novel in which one character is described as never having been quite the same since he opened a door and found himself in the middle of the last act of *La Traviata* and unable to get off the stage. The nearest I have seen to that is a boyar in *Boris Godunov* marooned trying to discover the parting in the curtains at the back of the stage as the action continued unabated.

Shakespearian productions seem more conducive than others to incidents of this kind. Once the lights went up to reveal Dame Edith Evans as Queen Katherine in *Henry VIII* arranged in the tableau with her ladies but, alas, in the dark her chair had fallen over backwards so that all the audience saw was the great actress's knees with foam rubber pads tied to them to enable her to kneel in comfort in the trial scene. She was not amused.

I have an affection too for a theatre-in-the-round production of *Hamlet* at a New England summer school at which I was teaching. The house lights went down and we were on the battlements at Elsinore with Bernardo and Marcellus awaiting the ghost. We did not have to wait long, for in he came through one of the doors used by the audience, followed by two or three late-comers who resolutely followed him as though he were an usherette as he glided his way around the stage.

It is some comfort to know that such gaffes are as old as theatre itself. The trouble is that all we generally have is the official tidied-up accounts of events in the past and rarely an on-the-spot report. We have to guess what really happened by reading between the lines, and it took a long, learned article to point out that Queen Elizabeth I actually ruined an entertainment written for her by Sir Philip Sidney by awarding the prize to the wrong person.

Occasionally an outsider provides an hilarious picture, as

when saucy John Harington describes calamity pile on calamity at a masque for James I. Everyone, including the cast, was drunk. Plenty emptied her fruits into the king's lap and Peace was able to get on stage only by walloping anyone in the way with her olive branch.

The miracle of theatre in reality is how very little in fact does go awry, bearing in mind the enormous technicalities involved. What a tribute to all those we take for granted, from electricians and scene-shifters to stage managers and dressers. In any case the majority of mistakes anyway would entirely bypass the average onlooker. In this I am reminded of Sybil Thorndike's account of playing Lady Macbeth opposite Lionel Barrymore in 1919. He apparently did not know his lines. 'I hurled him across the stage', she said, 'shouting them in his ear.' Probably no one noticed. She had been lent for the occasion the famous dress adorned with beetles' wings which we see in the Sargent portrait of Ellen Terry. The latter had told her: 'Don't worry. The dress will see you through.' It did.

Curtain Calls

IT IS SOMETIMES regrettably true that curtain calls can be more interesting than the two or three hours which precede them. Few things are more fascinating than watching the reactions of people who are the subject of applause. How surprising it must be for those, like the Princess of Wales, who suddenly graduate into the league of being able to evoke a state of instant euphoria in everyone without apparently having done a thing.

Two masters of the theatrical curtain call are Nureyev and Sir Frederick Ashton. Nureyev one remembers as just standing there alone in the middle of the stage, rather far back. He can walk forward but he is usually motionless apart from the bow of the head and, from time to time, the ultimate gesture of drawing, with one sweep of his right arm, the whole audience to him, extending his hand across his heart. Ashton is far more complex, beginning *piano* by being drawn in from the wings by a ballerina. This rather coy opening as the tidal wave of applause washes over him leads to a succession of stylized hand movements like the petals of an exotic blossom opening and closing in response to some unknown source of titillation. Even when he embraces on stage, the faces of the recipients are cupped between a sinuous arrangement of both hands.

Dietrich's curtain calls must have been rehearsed down to the last detail. Like Nureyev she stood alone, using very few movements, seemingly a statue entrapped in a sea of waves of silver fox fur lapping around her feet. There was the languorous hint of exhaustion of an ambiguous kind and the head of hair, of a colour, as was said of the first Elizabeth, of a colour never known to nature, raised and lowered itself as though by some invisible mechanism.

In these instances of theatre the control of illusion by way of the curtain and fall of light is critical. In the concert hall the approach has to be more prosy and is all coming and going. In only one instance have I witnessed that same sense of brilliant calculation. Herbert von Karajan came and went, seemingly impassive to the rapture he evoked, and then, in a final gesture, he strolled on wearing his overcoat, carrying his hat and walking stick. And that was that.

The fact of the matter is that these ritual exhibitions give as much pleasure to the audience as to the object of adoration. Acclamation of heroes and heroines fulfils a basic instinct in human nature. Only in time of war or great crisis does it ever extend into the political arena in this country where there is a fundamental distaste for the fascist cult of the leader in vast stage-managed spectacles. The British are able to channel that impulse around members of the Royal Family.

Whether they like it or not, all its members are cast, as James I wrote, as actors upon a stage whose tiniest gesture is observed. Their public life is one long curtain call which must be responded to by movement of the body and facial expression. None has eclipsed the Queen Mother as the mistress of this art, knowing the exact moment when to acknowledge the crowd by a lift of her arm or when suddenly to look back at them.

I was never more struck by this artistry than at the gala for her eightieth birthday at Covent Garden. After the interval she seemed to vanish from the grand tier. The audience began to wonder what had happened when suddenly a beam of light fell on the old royal box and a glittering figure slowly advanced, alone, to what became a tumult. As I looked I was reminded of Graham Robertson's famous description of Ellen Terry trying to arrive at a party unnoticed but in effect making an entrance like a sunrise.

The exponents of this art are few. They have the ability to seize hold of that magic moment when the routine acknowledgment of applause lifts itself by a kind of empathy into an art form of its own, leaving an indelible impression on the fortunate spectator.

Sir Frederick Ashton

FEW PEOPLE in the arts in this country can have given so many so much pleasure and delight as Sir Frederick Ashton. It seems only a short time ago that there was the great gala at Covent Garden when he retired as director of the Royal Ballet. Even then the roll call of his ballets projected on to a front cloth seemed never ending. It was an event when those of a younger generation saw brief snatches recreated from his earlier works, such as Margot Fonteyn in *The Wise Virgins*, which has long since vanished from the repertory.

Like so many, I was first aware of Ashton's work in the post-war era when what was to become the Royal Ballet moved to Covent Garden. That was a period when every year produced its fresh crop of books of photographs of the productions and of the dancers, then presented as cult figures in a way that was to be abandoned in the 1960s.

In these publications there would always be a photograph of Ashton, usually amid a clutter of Edwardiana, stretching up his profile towards a sepia print of Queen Alexandra in a silver frame. The portrait photographs of Ashton would indeed make a study in themselves right down to the recent panorama of him seated in his topiary garden. This carefully composed public persona is, of course, an essential aspect of the man.

So too are his abilities as a wit and courtier. Few people can excel him at mimicry and mime. It is the movement of his hands and fingers that most stick in my mind.

Over a decade ago I remember pointing that out to the formidable Mrs Ian Fleming at one of the gatherings over which she presided with an apparently permanent look of disapproval. David Hockney was there and I suggested what a marvellous sitter Ashton would make. One of the drawings that resulted is now in the National Portrait Gallery.

Ashton's social accomplishments make him an avid observer of *le monde*, with a facility to pinpoint character in a few words and a wave of the hand. No one can rival his ability to tell a member of the Royal Family how, in the past, she would have descended in a cloud machine to dance a ballet, or describe Gertrude Lawrence making an entrance, or offer to give the present Lady Dufferin lessons in how to manipulate her train as a marchioness. All this is allied to a droll *langueur* that is difficult to reconcile with such an abundance of work.

Ashton is a master of the mask and the face, for behind the former lurks the latter, which alone can explain the potency of his creations. They stem from wide reading, a deep feeling for the movement of the passions and an eagle eye for the follies and foibles of mankind.

These qualities are aligned to a typically British use of the romantic and modernist modes not as two opposites but as twin aspects of the same thing. Such a dialogue with styles in the arts which are imports from the mainland is as old as England. The adoption of the new wave is always piecemeal or layered onto the native tradition, like a palladian window added to an Elizabethan manor house.

That touches on the essential Englishness of Ashton, which is not true of his successor, MacMillan. One feels, for instance, as though Ashton's *Sleeping Beauty* descended to us from Tzarist Russia and Diaghilev via the court masques of Stuart England. A ballet like *The Dream* draws on layers of allusion from Shakespeare and Victorian romanticism to the native feeling for natural phenomena and liking for rich Hogarthian humour.

Façade, in retrospect, becomes the expression of the ethos of a period, the dance equivalent of E. F. Benson's magnificent Lucia. This richness explains why such ballets have taken on the status of classics.

It is, however, the great *pas de deux* that haunt the imagination. They are always placed at the true heart of his ballets, and provide the supreme moment when it seems as though a wand had been waved and time stood still as Oberon and Titania or Natalia Petrovna and Beliaev dance. All around one senses the audience catch its breath in sheer wonder. What greater legacy could one man's genius give us?

The Revival of Elgar

As I LEFT church the other Sunday, a neighbour smiled and said she was still in a haze from the celebration in Hereford Cathedral to mark the fiftieth anniversary of Elgar's death. Memories of that composer run deep in the Herefordshire-Worcestershire countryside. The widow of his organist lives in the neigbourhood; he is supposed to have visited our house, and he had, we were told, a reputation for pinching the maids.

I don't think anyone in the post-war period could have predicted the enormous resurgence of interest in his music that was to occur in the 1970s, or that he was to emerge as such a cult figure. For, like so many people in the arts, Elgar the person, the reality, is so different from Elgar the myth, the idea. In the long run it is the latter which matters, for he now occupies an unassailable position in our national musical mythology akin to that of Handel.

In 1952, my wife, who was then a student at the Royal College of Art, did the outline and designs for a ballet based on the *Enigma Variations*. Sir Hugh Casson arranged for these to be left at the stage-door of the Royal Opera House to be seen by Dame Ninette de Valois. Six months later my wife collected them, not thinking that they had been seen by anyone until, more than a decade later, Sir Frederick Ashton telephoned her to say that the time was right to do the ballet. This, in itself a romantic story, was accompanied by the comment that in the mid-1950s the pendulum had not swung in that direction. The triumphant reception of the masterpiece in 1968 inaugurated the upward curve of the Elgar graph. In the same year Michael Kennedy published his biography.

At first glance it is odd that as the swinging 1960s entered their apogee this should be so. In retrospect, however, it is hardly surprising. Although there had been a post-war neo-Edwardian revival in men's clothes and in interior decoration, it had certainly not extended beyond that. One thinks of Norman Parkinson's photograph of three dandies in their curled bowlers and velvet-collared coats. With that we were at the tail end of something which could never be put back. The Edwardian cult of the 1970s, in contrast, was never a style. It was nostalgia for what had become a vanished arcadia of peace and security before the First World War. The fact that the ballet still figures in the repertoire after 15 years is an index of the continuing potency of the image.

The revival of Elgar runs like a flood through the 1970s, and led to a revival of performances of his music abroad. Sir Adrian Boult's memorable appearances to conduct in his eighties were almost exclusively devoted to Elgar. The graph runs parallel with the obsession for the Edwardian age which, as the decade progressed, attained a crescendo in the gloom-laden years after 1974. It was a period marked by the rediscovery of life in the Edwardian country house, the film *The Go-Between*, Edwardian costume serials on television, an endless series of books of photographs depicting Edwardian England and its social life – even the society portraits of Sargent suddenly re-exerted their spell. In 1977 there appeared a book which at any other time would have sunk without trace but then sold in millions, *The Country Diary of an Edwardian Lady*.

Which brings me back to Elgar, for his music, above that by any other, is now locked into this distant, patriotic idyll of pre-1914 sunset splendour. The hostile Edward J. Dent in 1930 accorded only 16 lines to Elgar in a musical history compared to 66 to Parry and 41 to Stanford. He castigated his music as being 'too emotional and not quite free from vulgarity. His orchestral works ... are animated in colour but pompous in style and of too deliberate nobility of expression.'

That I cannot comment upon, for I am no musician. What interests me is the interrelationship of ideas and images that sustains the revival. In the 1960s when the promenaders burst into 'Land of Hope and Glory' in the midst of *Pomp and Circumstance*, there was a degree of mocking to the ritual. No one in recent years could make that accusation. That is because the references and allusions that his music evokes have changed over the years from being a symbol of imperial, insular, jingoism to Arcadian visions of the serenity of a golden age.

Fifty Years of Glyndebourne

My earliest memory of Glyndebourne was seeing it on television in the 1950s when, as an impoverished student, I was able to peer into this legendary world. Even the interval was filled by the camera just roaming over the audience strolling in evening dress or elegantly picnicking, the champagne corks popping. One felt like the peasantry peeping through a keyhole at a *fête champêtre* at Versailles.

That the vision was not a totally false one is confirmed by Cartier-Bresson's photograph of 1955. There, in a serpentining curve, ladies in long dresses clutching furs and men in black tie holding umbrellas wend their way across an expanse of lawn.

What is it that is so hypnotizing about Glyndebourne? I cannot claim to recollect more than 20 of the 50 years it now celebrates. Partly it might be thought its magic lies in the fact that it is almost impossible to get in. Rather more, however, surely resides in its alliance of opera with two things which haunt our imagination: the country house and the garden. It is unlikely that these factors ever crossed John Christie's mind as essential elements of its success but the quality of an extended country-house party is surely a key factor in the Glyndebourne success story.

It would be true to say that, if pressed hard, a high percentage of the audience would have to admit that what they really go for is the long interval. Although one recognizes a hard core of opera buffs, the audiences bear little resemblance to those at either Covent Garden or the Coliseum. On the whole they are made up of the comfortable City-commuting professional classes of Surrey and Sussex. Overheard conversation consists of unending eulogy rather than enlightened criticism.

Those who run Glyndebourne calculate such needs exactly: nothing contemporary, no shocks in productions of the classics and a careful recognition of the cultural timelag such an audience embodies. By that I mean that Glyndebourne adopts the new only when it has already been espoused elsewhere to the establishment pantheon.

The arrival of Peter Hall and David Hockney, for instance, make the point exactly. Both were *enfants terribles* in the 1960s but by the mid-Seventies emerged as the equivalent of Irving and Lord Leighton.

Glyndebourne's appeal also resides in the British love of amateurism. This does not in any way apply to its productions, but to the atmosphere. The auditorium is like a church hall and one's ticket is taken by ladies and gentlemen in evening dress as though it were a charity performance. Iced coffee and sandwiches in a makeshift tent heighten the ambience of a village fête; so too do the rambling buildings with glimpses of props and scenery and the sound of voices practising.

One very short-sighted academic summed it all up looking across the ha-ha to what was in fact a field full of black and white cows: 'How marvellous', he said, 'that the orchestra plays cricket in the interval.'

The smell of a Glyndebourne audience is of mothballs. Compared with Salzburg's bronzed, blonde, sharp chic, everyone cut from a page of *Vogue*, Glyndebourne is a parade of old fur and dresses that have seen better days. Apart from a sprinkling of frothy debs, the picture is of middle-aged, middle-class arthritic ladies in limp chiffon clutching shawls.

Only there could one see a lady in such dress, plus wellington boots, trudging across the turf.

The occasion is essayed with all the grim determination that the British have for alfresco events. Royal garden parties embody a similar display of mass masochism. In the case of Glyndebourne one's memory is that, like an army on the move, everyone is always carrying something – at least a programme, umbrellas, boots, picnic basket, folding chairs, rug and bottles. Watching the picnics is as enjoyable as anything else. Arrangements vary from hacking away at a loaf to a vast tableau of damask, silver and porcelain.

Glyndebourne is untransplantable. It is as English as a hollyhock or a lupin. It epitomizes all that makes and breaks the arts in this country: safety and snobbery, faded gentility and pretension, romance and dogged practicality, enchantment, perception and a certain visionary quality. May its magic never fade.